Eyes Only For Me

"Andrew Grey manages to take an emotional rollercoaster of a love story and turn it into a teaching moment."

—Prism Book Alliance

"A fascinating look deep into the hearts and minds of two men who never expected the discoveries they made along the way of changing and deepening their friendship to the point they become life partners."

—Rainbow Book Reviews

"This is a good story, with well written, well developed characters. There are some seriously hot, steamy scenes, and deeply profound dialogue between the main characters"

—Divine Magazine

The Lone Rancher

"As with many of Andrew Grey's stories, *The Lone Rancher* is a well written and easy read that leaves you with a HEA."

—The Novel Approach

Fire and Rain

"Andrew Grey continues to amaze me with his ability to write stories that will pull at your heartstrings and draw you into the world in which the characters live."

—Gay Book Reviews

"The characters will charm you and the plot... will... leave you with a smile on your face."

—Sinfully Gay Romance Book Reviews

More praise for
ANDREW GREY

Round and Round

"[Andrew Grey] built *Round and Round* with suspense, danger, loss and love, and with everlasting friendships and new beginnings."

—The Novel Approach

"…this book offered mystery, romance, friendship and a great group of characters."

—Inked Rainbow Reviews

The Gift

"Mr. Grey has given us a wonderful story of love and hope and I hope you each grab a copy and enjoy."

—House of Millar

Spirit Without Borders

"An emotional thrill ride with a lot of ups and downs... if you like passionate romances that are a little rough around the edges, this is a safe bet."

—TTC Books and More

"The realistic picture Andrew paints about the conditions, the area, the lives of these people grips you and you become emotionally involved in the story and you won't want to put it down until you finish."

—Rainbow Gold Reviews

By ANDREW GREY

Accompanied by a Waltz
Between Loathing and Love
Crossing Divides
Dominant Chord
Dutch Treat
Eastern Cowboy
Eyes Only for Me
In Search of a Story
The Lone Rancher
North to the Future
One Good Deed
Path Not Taken
Planting His Dream
Saving Faithless Creek
Shared Revelations
Stranded • Taken
Three Fates (Multiple Author Anthology)
To Have, Hold, and Let Go
Whipped Cream

HOLIDAY STORIES
Copping a Sweetest Day Feel • Cruise for Christmas
A Lion in Tails • Mariah the Christmas Moose
A Present in Swaddling Clothes • Simple Gifts
Snowbound in Nowhere • Stardust

ART
Legal Artistry • Artistic Appeal • Artistic Pursuits • Legal Tender

BOTTLED UP
The Best Revenge • Bottled Up • Uncorked • An Unexpected Vintage

BRONCO'S BOYS
Inside Out • Upside Down • Backward • Round and Round

THE BULLRIDERS
A Wild Ride • A Daring Ride • A Courageous Ride

BY FIRE
Redemption by Fire • Strengthened by Fire • Burnished by Fire • Heat Under Fire

Published by DREAMSPINNER PRESS
www.dreamspinnerpress.com

By ANDREW GREY (CONT.)

Published by DREAMSPINNER PRESS
www.dreamspinnerpress.com

By ANDREW GREY (CONT.)

WITHOUT BORDERS
A Heart Without Borders • A Spirit Without Borders

WORK OUT
Spot Me • Pump Me Up • Core Training • Crunch Time
Positive Resistance • Personal Training • Cardio Conditioning
Work Me Out (Anthology)

Published by DREAMSPINNER PRESS
www.dreamspinnerpress.com

Planting His Dream

Andrew Grey

DREAMSPINNER PRESS

Published by
DREAMSPINNER PRESS

5032 Capital Circle SW, Suite 2, PMB# 279, Tallahassee, FL 32305-7886 USA
www.dreamspinnerpress.com

This is a work of fiction. Names, characters, places, and incidents either are the product of author imagination or are used fictitiously, and any resemblance to actual persons, living or dead, business establishments, events, or locales is entirely coincidental.

Planting His Dream
© 2016 Andrew Grey.

Cover Art
© 2016 L.C. Chase.
http://www.lcchase.com
Cover content is for illustrative purposes only and any person depicted on the cover is a model.

ISBN: 978-1-63477-216-7
Digital ISBN: 978-1-63477-217-4
Library of Congress Control Number: 2016900164
Published April 2016
v. 1.0

Printed in the United States of America
(∞)
This paper meets the requirements of
ANSI/NISO Z39.48-1992 (Permanence of Paper).

Prologue

A Year Ago

"FOSTER," ARTHUR Galyon called from the back door of the old farmhouse that Foster's family had called home for generations. At least Foster was the third generation. But Foster wasn't sure how much he actually wanted to be a farmer, and he would have to make his decision soon.

"Yeah, Dad," Foster called back, looking up from where he'd been hiding for ten minutes in the equipment shed, behind the tractor, hoping for a few minutes of quiet. Very few cars passed their farm, and the only sounds were the animals in the field and the wind, but dang it, his father never gave him two minutes to himself. He set his copy of *Left Hand of Darkness* on the shelf and stepped out, wiping his hand on a rag so his father would think he'd been doing something.

"We need to get corn for the herd. Take the truck, get a load, and drop it in the field to augment the grass for the heifers." He turned to go back in the house.

"What will you be doing?" Foster asked. Yeah, his father would hate it, but Foster deserved to know. He was doing a lot of the work around the farm.

"What?" his father asked.

Foster walked over to his father. "I do a lot of the work here, and you know it." He placed his hands on his hips. This had been coming for a while, and on the spur of the moment, he decided it was time he stood up for himself. "I'm not a child, and I pull more than my share of the load around here. Always have, and you know it. So if you want something, ask, don't bark."

1

"Under my roof—" his father started, and Foster stepped closer, staring daggers into his father's blue eyes, which were mirrors of his own.

"Don't even say it," Foster interrupted. "I have opportunities away from this farm. So you need to decide the kind of relationship we're going to have and whether you want me as partner on the farm or not. So I'll ask again: What are your plans for the afternoon?" His father had always run the farm and the family with more control than Foster thought was necessary.

"If you think you can deliver an ultimatum to get out of your work…."

"When have I ever gotten out of work? I went to school and still managed to get my chores done, even driving into Muskegon so I could go to community college. Did anything change? Did my chores get done?" he challenged. "You know they did."

"What do you want?" his father asked suspiciously.

"I want you to stop acting like an ass," Foster said flatly. "I want you to treat me as an adult, someone who can make decisions and doesn't need to be told every damn thing that needs to be done. And dammit, stop acting like a dairy-farm drill sergeant. You aren't in the Army and haven't been for twenty-five years. And just so you know, I'm not some private you can bust down. I'm your son." Foster held his father's gaze, waiting to see his reaction. He figured there were two possibilities. The most likely was that his father would yell, threaten, and then pull rank, ending with his "under my roof" crap. Foster had heard that before. The other was to simply go inside, ignore what Foster had said, and pretend the words had never been heard. Arthur Galyon rarely changed anything for anyone. Everything was done his way, no highway option.

"Fair enough," his father said. Foster blinked twice, making sure he'd heard correctly. "I'm going to go to my office because I need to finalize the sale of the asparagus crop that's about to come in. A family is coming in to help with the harvest starting tomorrow, and I need to arrange delivery and make sure the buyer knows that the produce is coming. That way we can get paid faster."

"All right. Do you want me to direct the cutting this year or are you going to do it?"

His father hesitated. "You do it, and your mother and I will handle the morning milkings."

"Sounds good." Foster turned away and got in the truck, then headed out toward the last of the silos. They planted a huge amount of corn that they siloed in order to get the milk herd through the winter. The silos were now getting close to empty, and what was left had been on the bottom of the cylinder since last fall, so he'd have to heft it out and into the back of the truck. He'd only need a single load. Now that the grass was returning in force, they only used silage to supplement the grass and to try to keep some consistency in the herd's diet.

He backed up the truck to the silo, pulled open the door, and began pitchforking load after load into the back of the truck. The corn smelled sweet and a touch fermented. He loved that smell. It was one of the first ones to imprint on his memory, and he knew, no matter what, that this scent would always remind him of home. He was sweating by the time he got the back of the heavy-duty long-bed Ford completely filled.

Once he was done, he drove around and was surprised to find his father waiting by the gate. He opened it, and Foster drove through and continued on. He drove in a long arc around the edge of the field, getting out every so often to shovel some of the feed onto the ground. He stopped half a dozen times so the herd wouldn't congregate in one spot. Once he was done, he exited the pasture and parked the truck in its usual spot.

He got out and walked around the side of the house to where his mother had her garden. She and his father's mother were checking on tomato plants and strawberries, making sure the beds stayed weed-free. It was a constant chore.

"I hope we get rain," his mother said, looking up at the sky.

"I'll set one of the large impulse sprinklers out here when you're done. I'm hoping for rain tomorrow, but the plants are too tender to wait."

"Thank you," his grandmother called from where she sat, plucking the weeds from her strawberry patch. Foster walked over and gave her leathery cheek a kiss. His grandmother had spent her entire life on farms, and her skin showed it. Years of sun had taken their toll, but she was healthy as a horse and nothing stopped her.

"Are we going to have a good crop this year?" he asked.

"I think so." She groaned as she got to her feet. "Can we enlarge the bed? I've got lots of babies that we can transplant to fill the space."

"I'll get the tiller in a minute, and we can rake it out once the sun gets a little less hot. Then you can transplant as much as you want."

"What are we going to do with more berries?" his mother asked Foster. "We already put up enough jam and preserves."

"Mrs. Ruskin hailed me last week. She said it was just her and Mr. Ruskin now. She cleaned out her second chest freezer and asked if I wanted it. I helped get it out of her house, and it works, so I put it in the equipment shed yesterday. Dad and I can move it to the basement, and you and Grandma can fill it with berries to your hearts' content. She bought it four years ago from Sears—I know because I helped her bring it in. So it's good." That put an end to the discussion and put smiles on both women's faces. Dad would probably pitch a fit about the electric bill, because it was what he did, but Foster knew they made it through the winter on everything they could grow and put up from their own garden.

He got the tiller and began chewing up the ground along the side of the strawberry patch. The grass in that area was fairly decent, but it was on the side of the house and there was plenty of room to expand the bed. Using the machine was akin to riding a bronc. It bucked and shook and tried to run away with him sometimes. Foster made four passes and retilled the area a second time before putting the tiller away. By the time he got back, his grandmother was already chucking clumps of sod to the edge of the bed, humming to herself.

"She loves those berries," his mother said indulgently. Foster didn't blame her. His grandmother's heirloom strawberries were a huge deal to her. She had brought the first plants to the farm when she moved here with Grandpa after they'd married. They were an old variety and the best strawberries ever. Unlike the ones in the stores, these weren't big, but they were juicy and full of flavor. Foster got a rake and helped his grandmother by starting at one end, raking it out so she could start her transplanting.

In Michigan, the days were long in June, thank goodness, because there was always more work than anyone could get done. He'd just finished raking, his arms aching, when an old van pulled into the drive. A man, a woman, and three teenagers ranging from about thirteen to eighteen or so climbed out. "Can I help you?" Foster asked. He leaned his rake on a nearby fence and walked over to them.

"We're the Ramos family. We inquired about picking your asparagus. I'm Carlos. This is my wife, Maria, and my children, Ricky, Daniela, and my oldest, Javi."

"It's nice to meet you." He held out his hand. "I'm Foster. My father told me you'd be starting tomorrow." He looked at the van and wondered if they planned to stay in it, but said nothing. He'd learned that there were times when it was better to remain ignorant. They needed work, and his family needed the crop brought in.

His father came out and joined them, going over the details of the work and how they would be paid. They seemed agreeable. "We have an electric hookup near the field if you'd like to use it, along with water."

"That's much appreciated." That confirmed what Foster had thought.

"My son can take you out and show it to you. He'll be overseeing the work, so if you have any questions, you can speak with him." Arthur went back inside, and Foster explained where they were going. Then he climbed into the truck and led the Ramos family out of the drive and down the road about a mile to the edge of the asparagus field. He turned off the paved road onto a dirt track and stopped at the back corner of the field, near the trees. "The power is at the pole, and the water is in the shed." Foster unlocked both so they could have access. "There's also a fire ring if you want to use it, and the trees at the edge of the wood are on our property, so you can gather as much wood as you like." This was the first time he'd managed the harvest like this. He knew what was here, but the actual spartan living conditions of the people who would be working for his family had never hit home before.

"This is great. Thank you," Carlos said.

Everyone seemed to have their job and knew what to do. The younger teenagers retrieved an awning from inside, strung it to the edge of the van, and put it up. Carlos and Javi hooked up the electricity, and Maria set up tables and chairs outside, all within a matter of minutes.

"What time do we start?" Javi asked.

"I'll be here at seven with the tractor." They had an attachment for the back of the tractor with belts and adjustable platforms that allowed the workers to lie on their bellies. The tractor moved forward slowly, and as the asparagus was cut, it was placed on the belt and ended up on a tub in the center. It saved days of bending over. "We'll get everything set up and go to work."

"Is this the only field?" Javi asked.

"No. This is one of three. We'll pick each field twice in a rotation, with this one first. It takes a day per field."

Javi nodded and looked out over where the heads of the plants were sticking out over the ground. "So it's only six days."

"Actually two weeks. We pick for three days, and then we have to wait for more shoots, so we wait three or four days and then pick the second time." He made a note to ask what the pickers did in between. He did know if there was no work, there was no pay.

"I see." Javi didn't turn to look at him. "So we'll be here two weeks." He shook his head and then turned back toward the van that was the family's home. Javi had eyes as dark as night and twice as deep, skin as warm as the sun on his back. He was tall, but not too tall, and broad; strong, but not bulky like Foster—a body that was the result of hard work.

Javi was handsome, maybe more than handsome. Foster knew he shouldn't be having these thoughts about one of the workers on the farm, but his mind wandered a little and he had to pull it back so he was no longer wondering what lay under Javi's jeans and flannel shirt. "I should be heading back to the farm. Do you have a phone?"

Javi turned to him, eyes stormy.

"I'll give you my number so you can call if you need anything," Foster added in a hurry so Javi wouldn't think he was being insulting. Foster told Javi the number, and Javi wrote it down. Then Foster turned and said good night to the rest of the family before getting in his truck. He drove home, arriving in time to help his father with the evening milking.

It was dark by the time he got the milking done and sprinkler set in the vegetable garden, so he went inside, washed up, and sat down at the table. His mother brought him a plate, and Foster dug in, eating heartily. He was always hungry as soon as food hit his stomach. After years of working hard from sunrise to sunset, his stomach came alive when he let it. Usually he grabbed food and took it to go when he was working.

"Thank you for my bigger strawberry patch," his grandmother said as she came into the kitchen and sat down next to him.

"Did you eat?" he asked.

"Yes." She accepted a mug from his mother. After waiting until Foster's mother left the kitchen, she leaned forward and said, "I heard you and your father had a… discussion."

"Sometimes you have an interesting way with words."

"Your father wants what's best for the farm."

"Yes. But he's a tyrant sometimes, and if he wants my help, then he needs to appreciate it. You've been telling me that I needed to take the reins as an adult, so I have."

His grandmother nodded.

"He needs to recognize it," Foster said. "I'm not asking for anything that I'm not worth."

"I know. Your father takes after his father. I loved your grandfather, but he ran both the farm and your father."

"But I'm not him, and I'm trying to decide what I want to do with my life. I know Dad and Mom want me to stay and take over the

7

farm. It's what all of you have told me since I could walk. But I have to decide for myself." Foster finished his dinner and took the plate to the sink. His father and mother were in the living room, resting. "I'm going outside. I need to turn off the sprinkler."

His grandmother nodded and went to the sink to take care of the dishes. Foster knew she wouldn't go to bed until the kitchen was clean.

Outside, he turned off the sprinkler, then wandered over to where the herd was moving near the edge of the field. They stomped and lowed in the darkness.

Someone was out there, behind him. He heard footsteps and felt their presence. Darkness reigned in the country at night, and the only light came from the floodlight on the milking barn. "Can I help you?" He began heading back toward the house.

"Foster?" a tentative voice said, and then Javi stepped out of the darkness.

"What are you doing here?" Foster asked, approaching warily.

"I went for a walk and got lost. I thought I'd turned around to go back, but I got mixed up. When I saw the lights here, I thought I'd ask how to get back."

Foster relaxed. "Come on. I'll take you. I bet your mom and dad are worried."

"Not really. If it were one of the younger ones, they would be, but they'd only be concerned about me if I didn't show up to work." The resignation in Javi's voice made Foster wonder what kind of homelife Javi had. Foster pulled open the truck door and waited for Javi to get in. Once the doors were closed, Foster started the engine.

"Do you move around the country a lot?" Foster asked, more for conversation than anything.

"Yes. We were in Ohio a few weeks ago and have more work lined up here. We hope. Then, later in the summer, we'll start moving south again. Asparagus, beans, cherries, blueberries, apples, lettuce. We pick everything."

Foster glanced over at his passenger as he made the turn onto the road. He expected Javi to watch where they were going, but his gaze was straight at him, heated and intense. Javi turned away quickly. "At least you get to see a lot of the country." Foster had to say something, even if it sounded lame.

"I see nothing but fields and the van we live in." The yearning in Javi's voice made Foster apply the brake slightly without thinking. Damn, he wanted his father to treat him better, but he at least had choices in his life. He could see Javi had very few.

Foster approached the field, the dim light from the van off to the side. He pulled to a stop but didn't open his door. There were so many things he wanted to ask, but he couldn't think how to start.

"Thank you," Javi said, and then, to Foster's surprise, Javi touched his hand. Not for more than a few seconds, but long enough to shoot tingling heat through him. He'd never understood that a simple touch could shoot fire, good fire, through him. Almost before he could think about it, the touch was gone and Javi had his door open. Foster wanted to ask what had just happened, but it seemed too late, and what if it was his imagination? Better to keep it to himself.

"I'll see you tomorrow," Foster said, and Javi nodded before closing the door. Foster waited until Javi disappeared into the darkness before turning around and driving home.

CHAPTER 1

A YEAR—THE world could change a lot in a year. At least, Foster's outlook had certainly changed after spending two weeks around Javi. He hadn't done anything more than watch, but it had been enough to fire his imagination for months after the stunning young man and his family had left for their next job. Not that any of that really mattered now. Meeting Javi had spawned an awakening of self-awareness for Foster, but that had all been pushed aside. It didn't matter now; so little mattered now. The choices Foster had hoped to have had all changed too.

"Foster, come inside," his grandmother said gently from the kitchen door.

"I need to take care of the cows," he said, even though it was too early for milking. He needed something to take his mind off the weight—like his shirts were all lined with lead—that had settled on his shoulders in the past three days.

"I'll take care of it, Foster," Mr. Armitage said gently. He had a dairy farm a few miles away and had been one of his father's good friends. "Go on inside and see to the guests. Your mom and grandmother need you now." He placed his hand on Foster's shoulder. "Don't worry about things out here."

That was just it. Things out here were familiar and hadn't changed. It was everything inside the house that had changed. But he nodded and turned anyway. "Thank you." There would be plenty of chances for him to milk the cows. Twice a day milkings stretched out in front of him like a road heading straight through the middle of the rest of his life.

He pulled open the back door and went into the kitchen. The house was full of people all speaking in hushed tones. His mother sat on the sofa, talking quietly to one old family friend after another, a revolving place for everyone to pay their respects to the person left behind. He went in search of his grandmother and found her at the sink.

"Grandma, what…?" he said softly.

"This helps me feel like things are normal," she whispered. "Go on in there and talk to people. They've been asking after you, and believe it or not, they're here to try to help."

"Dad is still dead, and it doesn't matter what happens in there. He'll still be gone."

"Yes, he will, and I will have lost a son and you a father. But it helps to talk and to share stories. It's part of the grieving process." Her lower lip quivered, and Foster gathered her into his arms and let her cry against his shoulder. Tears welled in his eyes, but they dried up quickly. He wasn't going to blubber all over the place. He was the man of the family now, the one who had to see to it that his mother and grandmother were taken care of.

When his grandmother's arms clasped around his waist, he stood still and let her take whatever comfort she needed. Foster wasn't ready for comfort. All he kept seeing and feeling was how he wasn't ready for the responsibility life had just dropped at his feet. But it was there anyway, and he had to pick it up and run with it. "It's going to be okay, Grandma."

"A woman should never outlive her children. It hurts way too damn much," she said, and all Foster could do was nod in agreement.

"Katie," his mother said from the sofa, and Foster guided his grandmother over and helped her sit down. He stepped away, and before he realized it, he was engulfed and brought into a conversation with a number of his father's old cronies.

"They're expecting the price of corn to rise again," Greg Sharpton said. "That's going to hurt like hell when we have to buy feed, and if the price of milk goes any lower, we'll all be out of

11

business." He was in his midforties, and every time Foster had seen him, he'd always been full of gloom and doom.

"No one can predict the future," said Mark Hansen, the youngest of the group.

"That's easy for you to say—you grow your own corn." Sharpton turned to Foster. "You do too."

"Greg, we aren't here to talk about the doomed farm economy," the oldest man of the group, John Dulles, added. "Yes, things are a challenge right now. We can't keep doing the same things and expect to have roses at the end of the day."

"What are you saying?" Sharpton asked.

"Diversify. That's what you need to do," Mr. Dulles said. He was in his sixties and had done very well. How he'd done it had been a secret of sorts, and Mr. Dulles rarely said anything about his finances or his business. "I made a plan years ago, and it came to fruition." He stepped away, and the others continued their conversation. Foster wasn't really interested, so he stepped away as well.

He checked on his mother and grandmother, who were talking and seemed all right. Mrs. Dulles was sitting with them and had brought them plates from the grief buffet that had the dining room table groaning under its weight.

"I thought you could use this," Mr. Dulles said, pressing a coffee mug into his hand. Foster looked into the mug and had never been so thankful to see beer in his life. "Have you made any plans?"

Foster shook his head. There hadn't been time to think.

"That's fine. You will." He moved Foster to the side of the room. "You're going to be flooded with people who have advice or are willing to help you by taking the farm off your hands. They may even throw what sounds like a lot of money at you." Mr. Dulles sipped from his mug, and Foster wondered if there was beer in that one as well. "Don't do it. The land you have here is worth a great deal. The fields are some of the best in the county, and the acres of asparagus are priceless. No one else has anything like that, and if they wanted to plant, it would take years before anything was ready."

"But what do I do?"

"Take stock of what you have, both good and bad, confirm your financial position, and then diversify. Sharpton will say farming is an art, but he's full of it. Hansen will tell you it's a science and that you should watch weather patterns and crap like that. But farming is a business, and you need to run your farm as a business. Cash flow, accounting, all that. You have products to sell and you need to get the most from them. Some people, like me, go big and produce on a large scale. I have quality product at a low cost per unit, and I command a good price for my chickens as well as the eggs." He looked around. "We also sell at some farm markets. People come every week to buy what we have, and they pay retail for it. Don't underestimate how much that can save your ass."

"I can't take milk to market," Foster said.

"No. But you can take other things that will generate cash. Think of the farm as a business first and make your decisions that way." He looked over at the group of men still carrying on their discussion. "I can't tell you what you should do, but if you want some advice later, or just want to talk, I'll certainly listen."

Mr. Armitage came over and nodded to Foster before joining their little group. "The herd is fine, and the barn is all set for tonight's milking. The dairy came and I supervised the testing and loading of the milk. They'll be by again tomorrow, of course."

"Thank you." Foster was definitely more than a little out of it at the moment. He sipped from his mug, the hoppy brew bracing him and helping to open his eyes.

"You need anything, you let me know. This is a large place to run on your own," Mr. Armitage said.

"I appreciate the advice and the offer," Foster told him. "I've been doing a lot of the work for a while now." He took another drink. "Dad had been slowing down a lot over the past few months. I thought it was him getting a little older and stepping back to let me run things." He swallowed. "Now we know it was his heart." The damn fool hated doctors and hadn't gone, even though his mother had asked him to go many times.

"Well, we're all here for you," Mr. Armitage said and shook Foster's hand before gathering his wife and saying good-bye to Foster's mother and grandmother.

"Farmers help each other, but nobody is going to work your land for you," Mr. Dulles said. "And you know as well as I do that Frank Armitage has had his eye on this farm and land since your dad refused to sell it to his dad when your grandfather passed. There's a lot of history in this room—some good, some not. You hear me?"

"Yes. What about you? Do you want the farm too?"

"No. I have my business. And yes, I'd buy your farm and turn most of it into fields where I could grow feed. That's what I need, but that isn't the best use of this particular land. So I don't have my eye on your farm the way others do." He clapped Foster on the shoulder. "Don't concern yourself with any of that. You worry about running your business the way it needs to be run. You're young, but you have a lot of experience in your mother and grandmother." He smiled slightly. "I'm going to get another piece of that chocolate pie before it's gone."

Foster thanked him and stood alone after he'd walked away. He drank the rest of the beer and thought about going in search of some more to take the edge off.

"Foster," his mother called gently, and he went over to her. "I forgot to tell you that those people are coming in two weeks, the ones who picked for us last year. Your father must have made the arrangements."

"I'll take care of it." He patted her hand. He still had to go through all his father's notes to figure out what plans he'd made and to pick up on what was yet to be done, and this was just another item to add to his list. But first he had to get through what was left of this day.

An hour later, Foster said good-bye to the last of the guests. His mother and grandmother appeared ready to fall over. "Thank you, Mrs. Dulles, for all your help." She'd packed away the last of the food that had been brought and then said good-bye.

Finally. Foster pulled off his tie and loosened his collar. "I'm going up to change and then take care of the milking."

"I'll help you."

"No, Mom. Go and put your feet up, rest. The past three days have been way too hectic."

"There's too much to do."

"But we don't have to do it all today." Foster hugged her and then went up to his room. He changed into jeans and a light long-sleeved shirt. Then he went out and let the first group of cows into the barn. They went right to their stalls, and Foster cleaned their udders and began putting on the milking machines. Powered by compressed air, the machines did the time-intensive work, with the milk flowing directly through pipes to the collection vat. His job was to keep the milking machines moving. He had a limited number, so he transitioned them every five minutes or so until the cows were done. Then he shifted the girls out of the barn and cleaned up the inevitable mess with a shovel and hose before bringing in the next group. The entire process took about two hours, and by the time he got back to the house, he was exhausted.

"Go up to bed," his mother said, but Foster instead went into his father's office to try to make sense of the records and where the farm stood financially.

The herd records were easy to find. His father had kept detailed records of all injections and treatments as well as parentage and so on. The financial records were another matter. It took more digging to find what he was looking for. As he was looking, he also found a life insurance policy that he hoped like hell was still paid up. He set the policy in the stack of things he needed to talk to his mother about.

Finally he got to the bank statements and was shocked. There was money in the bank—not a lot, but some. Probably enough to get them through to the fall. But it was the debts that shocked him. The farm had a mortgage, which didn't surprise him, but the others did. Even credit cards.

By the time he couldn't stay awake anymore, he had a really good idea of just how bleak their overall financial health—not just the farm, but his family—really was. What scared the hell out of him was that this was what he knew about. There had to be more he hadn't found yet.

Concerned and scared, but too tired to think straight, Foster went upstairs and got into bed. It would all be there in the morning, and he'd need to work out how to pay all the debts off.

CHAPTER 2

THE NEXT few weeks didn't make things easier.

"Mom," he said softly as he sat at the dining room table where his family had eaten for generations. It was old, heavy, huge, and as much a part of the family history as the rest of the farm.

"Your father had insurance," she said.

"Yes, and he left you and me as the beneficiaries, just like you and Dad added me to the farm a few years ago. But he's also been borrowing and spending on credit cards, and unless we use the life insurance money to pay them off, we're going to be eaten alive."

"How much is there, really?" she asked, and Foster passed over his calculations. "Forty-three thousand dollars?" She seemed as floored as Foster.

"I went online and looked at the past bills. There are things on the bills like last year's Christmas presents, and winter coats at two hundred dollars each." He passed over the bills. He was beginning to wonder what he'd find if he went into his mother's closet. "What have you been doing?"

"I go into Grand Rapids once a month and—" She stared. "I didn't know. He never showed me the bills."

"No. He just paid the minimum. He wanted to make you happy. The thing is, we have to pay all these off. So the hundred and fifty thousand from the insurance is one-third gone, like that. There's also the mortgage and the line of credit against the farm. We can't pay the mortgage off, but there's another fifty thousand in second-mortgage debt. So there goes another third. The rest we're going to need to make sure we don't slip back to where we were."

"Oh God." She put her hands over her face and began to cry.

"We'll be all right, but we have to be smarter."

"What should we do?" she asked.

Foster had given it some thought. "First thing, we're going to enlarge the garden, and I've found out there's a farmer's market in Grand Rapids each Saturday. It's well attended, and Mr. Dulles said he could help get us in. That means we're going to have to plan what we grow and sell a lot of what we produce. That will help with cash flow."

"Who's going to go?"

"You and Grandma. You can drive, and I'll have everything set up for you. It's one day a week, and it will get you away from here."

"What was that about me?" Grandma Katie asked as she joined them.

"We're going to sell our vegetables at the market. Foster thought you and I could do it," his mother explained.

"You bet your ass we can do it. I told my son we should have been doing that years ago, but he wasn't interested." There were times when Foster loved his grandmother. "We didn't build this farm to see it fail."

"But what about getting through the winter?"

"Harriet," his grandmother snapped. "We've got enough food put up to feed an army. Yes, we'll need some for ourselves, but we always have extra that we give to friends and pass on. Now we're going to grow more and sell all the extra."

"I think we're going to sell as much of the asparagus as we can, too. Dad was getting almost a dollar a pound for the whole crop, but in the store it's three to four dollars a pound. So we can take some of it to market and do well at two pounds for five dollars. I doubt we can sell the whole crop that way, but I bet we can sell enough to make some real money."

"Now that's thinking. When Harley planted those fields, he was thinking long term and knew he could make some money with it. They've been paying off for years," his grandmother said.

18

"And they will this year too." Foster was glad he had their support. "I was also thinking that you used to make cheese. I remember it as a kid."

"Yes, I used to, but I haven't in years." She looked up at him. "Honey, I'd love to try, but I don't have it in me any longer. I'll teach you how, though."

"I'll learn too," his mother said.

"I know this is going to be added work for us, but we'll be doing it for ourselves. Lately it seems we've been selling our products to a supplier or wholesaler, and the prices have gotten low enough that Dad wasn't able to break even. We have to somehow."

"What about sweet corn?" Grandma Katie asked.

"I planted a couple rows along the edge of the field closest to the house, like usual. When the harvest time comes, we'll use some and sell the rest." Now that he had an idea of how they could make extra money, he was ready to throw himself into it. "I don't know how much we're going to make, but if we don't try, we aren't going to get anything."

"Okay," his mother said. Clouds had begun to roll in, and she turned to his grandmother. "I think you and I need to get out to the garden. If it's going to rain, then the seeds need to be in the ground."

"I'll be right out. I'm going to make the garden as big as I can."

Lord help them all if this didn't work out. Vegetables were hard work, and with three of them instead of four, they would be stretched to the limit. His mother and grandmother would do what they could, but he'd have to make up any shortfall. He had no illusions about that. But he had to try because giving up wasn't an option.

Foster checked his watch and went out to get the additional feed for the herd. He delivered it and then helped his mother and grandmother in the garden. He tilled up an area that hadn't been used in a few years, so it had set well and was a chore. Then he started raking while his mother got her tomatoes planted and his grandmother planted her leafy veggies. They'd planned the garden in patches, and by the time thunder sounded in the distance, they had made really good progress.

"Hold off a little longer," Grandma Katie said as she looked at the sky.

"What about melons and pumpkins?" his mother suggested.

"Too fussy and we never get a good yield. Let's stick to what's always done well for us," Foster said, and his mother nodded her agreement.

In the end they planted extra spinach, green and yellow beans, and some squash for the fall.

"That ought to do it," his mother said.

Foster was exhausted, and so were his mother and grandmother, but everything had been planted, and the rain was coming any time. The women headed inside, and Foster went out to the barn. He let in the first group of cows and got them milking as the sky opened up. He knew the others were waiting out under the overhang that extended from the barn, so they'd be out of the worst of the rain.

The routine of milking gave Foster a chance to think. He'd put together a plan and hoped it paid off. If most things came to fruition in the garden, there would be way more than they could use, which would give them plenty to sell. By the time he was done milking, the storm had passed through. Moisture hung in the air and dripped from the eaves. Puddles had formed in the drive, but they would be gone fairly quickly. The important thing was that they had gotten a good rain, and with crops in the fields and the garden planted, that was the number one ingredient at the moment. That and his ability to stay ahead of the chores that needed to be done.

FOSTER WOKE up the following morning barely remembering that he'd slept. He shuffled down the stairs and into the kitchen. His mother and grandmother weren't up, which was surprising but not concerning. After how hard they'd worked, they must have been tired. Foster started the coffee and then went back upstairs to finish getting dressed. By the time he came down once again, the coffee was ready, and he drank his first cup of the day before heading out for morning milking. Once that was done and the truck had arrived to take delivery of the milk, he was ready for breakfast.

He reached the back door as a familiar van pulled into the drive. He paused at the door and then went over to meet them.

"I thought you were arriving next week," Foster said, hoping there wasn't a mix-up.

Carlos Ramos looked ragged and tired. The others looked even worse as they slowly climbed out of the van. The two younger ones had hollow looks and stayed close to their mother. Javi's eyes blazed with anger that seemed to be focused on his father.

"We…. Things didn't work out at our last job."

"I see." Foster wanted to ask the details, but he figured he probably wasn't going to get them. They had done a great job the year before. "Come on in and have some breakfast, and I'll give you the key so you can go set up. We can't pick for another week yet, but you can stay and get some rest if you like." Foster could tell Carlos was on the verge of saying no.

"Breakfast would be very nice," Maria said in a heavy accent. Foster tried to remember if she'd ever spoken to him before. Ricky and Daniela looked up at their mother in disbelief. Javi continued staring daggers at his father as Foster motioned them toward the house. There was an interesting dynamic playing out in front of him that he found curious, even if it was none of his business.

He led the way inside. Grandma Katie was already in the kitchen making breakfast. She took one look at the family that trooped in and began cracking more eggs and frying more bacon. The toaster got a heck of a workout, with his mother coming down and helping a few minutes later.

By the way they ate, Foster wondered just how long it had been since they'd had a good meal. All five of them tucked in, clearing everything on their plates. They thanked Foster and his mother and grandmother, saying very little while they sat at the table. Maria cleared the table and insisted on helping clean up. Carlos herded the others outside, and when Foster went out, he found them hauling and stacking the remains of one of the old buildings that had fallen during the winter. The building hadn't been used in years, and Foster hadn't had a chance to clean it up. But it seemed they were determined to work for their breakfast.

"Please be careful of any nails," Foster said gently. The job didn't take long and the jumbled mess was turned into a neat pile of debris. Maybe once it rained enough, he'd burn it all to get rid of it permanently. He didn't want the fire to get out of control.

"Here's the key," Foster said. "Do you remember the way to the field?"

"Yes," Javi answered, taking it. "Thank you." Somehow Foster got the idea he was being thanked deeply for a lot more than just the key or the food. Again, there was so much going on between father and son at the moment that Foster wondered if he'd been dropped in a production of Kafka. "I'll bring it right back." He pocketed the key, and they all gathered back inside the van. Once Maria joined them with a bag that his grandmother had no doubt given her, they backed out of the drive, and Foster watched the van disappear before getting to work.

The rain started in the midafternoon. He did what he could, but many of the items on his list were outdoor tasks. In the end, Foster made sure the herd had taken shelter and that they had feed, and then he retired to his father's office to recheck the bank accounts and make phone calls.

First he called the people who'd bought their asparagus crop the last few years.

"Justice Produce," a woman said.

"This is Foster Galyon, and I wanted to talk to someone about purchasing my asparagus crop."

"That would be Mr. Justice. Please hold a minute." The line went quiet for just a few seconds.

"Foster," Mr. Justice said with too much energy. "Is it that time of year already?" He laughed. Foster didn't get the humor, but the man apparently thought he was funny somehow. "I ran the numbers and can offer a dollar five a pound for your entire crop."

"Actually, I'm looking for a slightly higher price. The quality is excellent." He looked at the closed door to the office and cringed before plunging on. "I have someone interested at a dollar fifteen a pound, and I wanted to talk to you first before I accepted their offer. I'm only selling eighty to eighty-five percent of the crop. The rest we're going to take to market ourselves."

A squeak sounded in the background. "Your father never did that."

Foster shrugged even though no one could see it. "I'm not my father. Do we have a deal?" He'd never truly trusted this man, and from the instructions his father had left him last year about making sure everything was weighed before it was picked up, his dad hadn't either.

"Well...."

"If you can't...." Foster was becoming very afraid that he'd overplayed his hand. There wasn't another buyer, but it was a tactic Mr. Dulles had told him to use if he felt the need. He'd also explained that if it didn't work, Foster could be left with the unenviable task of going back later and getting a lower price than the original offer. And he was afraid he was seconds from being called.

"Let me see...." He knew Mr. Justice was stalling.

"I can just call...," he began, his heart pounding.

"No. I can do a dollar fifteen a pound for everything you're willing to sell." He sighed, and Foster knew he'd been right—his father had been underpaid for years. He pulled out the file he'd created for the crop and made a note to negotiate another buyer in the fall for an even better price. Maybe Meijer would buy it lock, stock, and barrel.

"Thank you," Foster said. "Dad always said to do business with people who treated us right in the past." His father had never said anything of the sort. "We're going to start picking next week, so I'll call to confirm the daily pickups. E-mail over the agreement, and I'll sign it and get back to you."

"Agreement?"

"Yes. Just to document our price. It's a good practice for both of us." Foster kept his voice light, but he was determined to have things in writing. That was the best way to protect himself and the farm. "I look forward to seeing it soon." He tried not to be nervous as he ended the call, sinking back into his chair and letting out a breath.

"What's going on in here?" Grandma Katie asked, poking her head in.

"I just got us fifteen cents a pound more than Dad was getting from Old Man Justice." He grinned as his grandmother came inside and sat down.

"You watch that man. He's slippery as an eel and has the heart of a snake. I knew his father, the old bastard. What he can't get one way, he'll try to get another. Greedy and heartless, the whole family."

"Well, I need to get the best price I can for all of us."

"Of course you do, just don't trust him."

"I told him to send an agreement."

She patted his hand. "You ain't no fool." Grandma Katie got up and went to the door. "You get that from me." He pulled the door closed after she'd left, then called the dairy as well as the veterinarian. A number of cows would be giving birth soon, and he wanted to make sure Dr. Martin was aware of what needed to be done.

"How are things going?" the veterinarian asked once they'd taken care of the immediate business.

"Overwhelming," Foster told him.

"You need to find a wife who understands the life of a dairy farmer and start your own family. You can't run the place on your own, and while your mother and grandmother can help, they can't take on that workload."

"I know."

"And you can't do it all yourself. You may try for a while, but things will get away from you. I've seen it before, and I'd hate for you to get sick or too run down to be productive."

"For now things are the way they are." It was the only answer he had, and there was no way on God's green earth he was going to marry someone, especially a woman, just so they could help him on the farm. He had no interest in women, not like that, but he'd always kept those thoughts to himself, and would continue to do so.

"Will you be in church on Sunday?" Dr. Martin asked.

"Yes. I'll bring Mom and Grandma after I finish the morning milking." Much of their non-farm life centered on the church. Foster had been attending the Church of Christ since he was a kid. It was where his parents went, so he'd gone. "Will I see you there?"

"If I don't have an emergency." A phone rang in the background. "I need to go, but I'll see you Sunday." He hung up and Foster did the same.

It was still raining, and from the looks of the radar app on his phone, it seemed to be settling in to do that for the rest of the day. Foster put on a raincoat and went out to the barn. He might as well get the inside work done. He hung up his coat once he was inside, then grabbed a shovel and cleaned out the residual dung before grabbing the hose.

"You wouldn't need any help?"

Foster jumped, dropping the hose. He hadn't expected anyone.

"Sorry," Javi said as he stepped forward. He was soaked to the skin, and Foster guessed he'd walked over. "I need some work." He shuffled his feet nervously. "Things have not gone well."

Foster had guessed that. "Can you hose down the floor and milking stations?" Foster wondered how Javi kept from shivering, but he picked up the hose and started cleaning everything. Foster went to work on the milking machines, making sure they were spotless. "Mop the floor in the milk room too." Foster figured he might as well get a leg up on his chores. He went to the loft and brought down some hay for the feeders along with the protein supplements. He added some silage, as well, to sweeten the mixture.

The rain had let up by the time he was done, and Foster pulled out his wallet and handed Javi some cash for the work he'd done. Javi shoved the bills into his pocket. Foster wanted to ask him what had happened and why they were so desperate, but the pride

Foster saw in Javi's eyes told him he could ask, but that answers wouldn't be forthcoming.

"Do you need help tomorrow?" Javi asked.

Foster wasn't going to be able to afford someone to help him all week, but he found himself nodding anyway. He knew his mother and grandmother would try to help them any way they could, so it was best to let Javi work and earn the money he needed to help his family. Foster knew that machismo, male pride, was huge in Latino culture. Getting Javi to take charity would be difficult. "If it's nice, the garden will need to be tended and weeded." After all the rain, what they'd planted would sprout overnight. "You can also help me shift the hay in the loft to help make room for the new cuttings."

"I'll get here early."

"Do you want a ride back?" Foster asked. Javi shook his head. He left the barn, jogged out to the road, and then down toward the field. Foster watched him the entire time, enjoying the smooth way he moved. He had to force himself to turn away. He shouldn't be having thoughts like this. He went back in the barn up to the loft and started the process of cleaning and shifting the hay. Moving the heavy bales was just the ticket to work away these thoughts about the gorgeous farm worker.

He retrieved the remaining wayward bales of hay from the edges and corners, placing them near the chute to the main floor, stacking them neatly and then going for more. Foster hated that he had these feelings. He'd heard since he was a toddler all about the evils of alcohol, smoking, and many more prohibitions from the front of the church. More than once he'd heard the prohibition about men lying with men and had sworn the minister had been looking right at him and could see into his soul. In the last year he'd been able to find a lot of chores that had to be done, so he hadn't been going to church as often. In a roundabout way, he felt better not hearing that he was a godless sinner all the time.

"Foster," his mother called up. "Your grandmother and I are going to town. Do you need anything?"

He checked his watch and realized he'd been working for hours. "Some snacks would be nice." He climbed down. "When will you be back?"

"About an hour. We'll make dinner then." She left, and Foster went about the process of getting ready for milking, thinking that this was a much easier job with two people, but it was only him, so he might as well get to it. Besides, the work gave him something to think about other than the same set of eyes, light caramel-brown skin, and full lips that had stayed in his mind now for nearly a year. Part of him wished that Javi and his family hadn't contacted his father about working. Then he wouldn't be reminded of how he felt and could go on with his life. Not that he knew if Javi felt the same way.

He let in the first half of the herd and started the milking process, noting the cows that were going to be getting ready to calve soon. He kept detailed records and made notes in his mind regarding when he'd need to separate them into the calving pens. The work never ended, and Foster got to it, finished the milking, cleaned up the barn, and went inside to have dinner. Afterward, he checked that everything was all set for the night, then spent a quiet hour before going up to bed.

That night, as he lay in his bed, staring at the ceiling, tired and worn out, his mind would not let up. All he kept seeing was Javi, worn and hungry-looking, at least to start. It didn't take long before his mind put Javi, not smiling, his eyes filled with heat, standing near him, pulling off his shirt and then tugging at Foster's. Javi pulled him close, their chests touching, breath heaving, lips finally exploring. The funny thing was that Foster had never kissed anyone the way Javi kissed him in his fantasies, like he was reaching down deep to Foster's heart and soul. As heated as he became, Foster shook his head and put a stop to his fantasy. This was not helping him. He needed to be strong.

Foster hated guilt. The animals he worked with all day never felt guilt about anything. They went about their day, crapped where they were, ate their food, sometimes nuzzled him when he put on the milker. Foster always talked to them and gave them a few pats. Of course he'd seen mothers with young, licking them and caring for them. The cows were simple creatures, and there were times when he wished he were as well. They felt no guilt over whatever they did, and yet something that seemed as innate and deep as the basic actions his cows did had been drilled into him as wrong. That seemed off to him, and he'd like to charge that those people, preaching what they didn't know about at all, were the ones who should be feeling guilty. Foster got up and went to the bathroom, getting a drink of water and trying to settle his mind.

He wasn't going to find any answers, certainly not in the next five minutes, and he needed to get some sleep. Foster willed all of the worries and the weight of the farm off his shoulders for the night and got back into bed.

"Honey," his mother said, knocking softly on his bedroom door. "Are you sick?"

That was a bad term, because the first answer that came into his head was that he was in the eyes of the church, but that wasn't what his mother had asked. "No, Mom." She opened the door and came in. "I couldn't sleep, that's all."

"Me neither. I haven't since…." She turned away. "I slept next to your father for twenty-five years. We didn't go places because we had the farm, so I can't remember a night we slept apart in all our married lives. Now the bed's way too big." Foster wasn't sure how much he wanted to hear about his parents' bedroom life, but if it did his mother good to talk, then he'd listen. "It's so unfair. Your father could be a control freak… as you've called him many times, but he did his best for all of us and worked hard his entire life."

"I know, Mom." One minute his father was there and the next he was dead just outside the milking barn, lying in the grass. That was it. He was gone.

"You know what I thought when they first told me? That it was a good thing he didn't die in the barn or they'd make us throw all the milk away." She covered her face and wept. Foster got out of the bed and held her, his fantasies long gone.

"Mom, we all think strange things when we're under stress."

28

"I know. But it took a few seconds to realize that he wasn't coming back. That I was going to be alone." She pulled away and wiped her face. "I'm acting like an idiot."

"No, Mom. You're grieving, and that's healthy." He didn't know what else to do other than try to comfort her. "All we can do is move on and take care of things as best we can."

"But you're twenty-three years old. You shouldn't have to shoulder the burden of this place alone. Not at your age. We had such plans. I wanted to send you away for a while, let you see some of the world before your life became the farm, with milkings two times a day and a business that was dependent upon something as fickle as the weather." She wiped her eyes again. "All I ever wanted for you was a life better than the one your father and I had, and it looks like you're going to have the exact same life we did."

Foster sighed. He doubted that very much. "Things will be different. My life will be different if I make it different." The words rang hollow in his ears, though. He was saying them without really believing them. Sure, he wasn't going to have a wife, but he would be milking cows and trying like hell to get through the lean years while making up for them as best he could when things went his way. He'd grown up here—he knew what life on a farm meant.

She looked into his eyes. "Do you remember how you'd always tell us whenever you got angry that as soon as you were old enough, you'd leave and never come back?"

"Yeah." It had been what he'd wanted at the time. Other kids in school played soccer and football after school; he went home and did his chores and then homework. Rain, shine, snow, freeze your nuts off—didn't matter. "At the time things didn't seem fair. Now I know they never are and aren't likely to be." In those few seconds, he thought about Javi. He was quickly becoming the stand-in for the things Foster wanted but knew he could never have. "We need to get to bed. The rain seems to have ended, and in the morning there's going to be plenty to do."

"The farm goes on," she murmured.

29

"It never stops." Even in the dead of winter there were chores to do and work that had to be done. But June was a time when there was more work than could possibly be accomplished. Granted, he didn't want his mother and grandmother doing more than they could handle, so he needed his sleep as much as she needed hers.

"Good night, then," she said and left the room. Foster got back in bed, and this time he was able to fall to sleep. Just the thought of the tasks ahead of him for tomorrow was enough to make him tired, and he dropped right off.

CHAPTER 3

FOSTER GOT up early, got his four-legged girls into the barn as soon as he could, and started the milking process. They made much more noise than usual. "I know. It's early for me, too, but I need to get things done," Foster said as he worked. "So wake up and have an early breakfast." He left the first group in the barn a little longer than usual to make up for getting started early and then put them out and brought in the second group. Once milking was done, he cleaned out the barn and got ready for the day.

"Did you sleep at all?" his grandmother asked when he came back inside. She was still in her nightgown and robe.

"Yes. But I was up early and got things done. It's going to be a great day, and I have some help for you in the garden," Foster explained.

She looked at him sideways. "Not that Rumston boy who came last fall and stayed one day, complaining how his arms hurt." She scoffed. "That kid's way too soft for this work."

"No. Javi Ramos."

She nodded. "When is he coming?" She shuffled toward the door. Foster knew she was starting to slow down. His grandmother was seventy and that was expected, but he hated to see it.

"I expect him anytime."

"Then I'm going to dress and get breakfast on. He needs to eat before we go out into the garden. I have some things I want to replant, and he can help me."

"What are you going to do?"

"Plant some flowers," she said. "I have some dahlia and gladiola bulbs in the basement. I put them in last year, but only to keep them

31

alive. I want to divide them and get them planted. I bet we can sell bouquets at your market if they grow well."

"Then go for it. We should be able to help." He smiled as she left the kitchen. Looking through to the living room window, he saw Javi walking up the drive. He wore jeans and a light shirt. When Foster went out to meet him, he realized just how threadbare the clothes were. In places the jeans seemed about ready to fall apart. Granted, they provided one hell of a view and left very little to the imagination. But Foster wasn't supposed to be looking at that.

"Grandma is making breakfast, so let's finish in the loft, and then she's going to need help in the garden." Foster also made a note to go and check all the fields he'd planted to see if the corn and alfalfa had sprouted. After the spring warmth and now the rain, the plants should be growing like crazy. There was so much going through his head, and he didn't want to forget anything, so the list kept playing on a loop. He hated when that happened, but it was how he kept things straight.

The semisweet scent of hay perpetually filled the air in the loft. Foster sneezed once, like he almost always did when he climbed into the loft. He sometimes thought it a strange habit his subconscious had picked up somewhere along the way.

Javi worked hard; Foster had no complaints about that. He didn't talk or shirk, moving bale after bale with nothing more than an occasional grunt. "Is this all there is?" Javi finally asked.

"Yeah. I'm using up the last of the winter stores. The grass has been growing well and will shoot up after the rain, so the cows will be in pretty good shape."

"What about next winter?" Javi asked.

"We'll start cutting hay next month, and if we're lucky, there will be three cuttings this year. Usually we do the last one as rolled bales, and I can tractor those into the pastures. The best hay I can usually trade with the horse farms because it's worth more than the cattle hay. Sometimes twice as much." Getting enough feed to last the winter was always a job, but Foster understood what had to be done, and he had the acreage to support the farming operations.

"Must be a lot of work," Javi said as he moved the last bale of hay onto the low stack near the door. The sun was already heating up the loft, and Javi's arms glistened with dampness.

"It is. Every winter is a balancing act. Set aside too much, and you end up having money tied up in what you don't need. Not enough set aside, and then I have to pay high end-of-season prices to get lower-quality feed." Even as he talked to Javi, he was starting to see how Mr. Dulles was right. Everything on the farm was money, from time, to feed, to supplies, to seed, to the land itself… and the taxes he had to pay. Fucking hell, no wonder farms and dairy operations were shutting down or selling out to bigger firms.

"I see," Javi said as he pulled a cloth from his back pocket and wiped his brow.

"Let's get down out of here." Foster motioned to the stairs and turned out the lights. As he descended, the air freshened with each step, cooling his overheated skin. The only problem was that as he went, he watched Javi, becoming entranced by the way his rear end bobbed slowly ahead of him. If he'd been paying attention, he wouldn't have knocked into Javi and then scrambled to get away and ended up flat on his ass on the floor. "Damn," he swore under his breath. The only saving grace was that he wasn't sitting in cow droppings. His butt hurt, but that was nothing compared to the rush that went right to his head when Javi took his hand and tugged him back to his feet. Touching a live wire hadn't sent such a jolt through him, and while the hair on his head didn't stand up, the hair on his arms certainly did.

"Are you hurt?" Javi asked in a tender tone.

"Just my pride." He felt stupid and released Javi's hand. His tailbone ached, but there was nothing he could do about it. "Breakfast should be about ready."

"Shouldn't we wash the barn out again?"

"I did that this morning already." Foster looked over the milking floor. "Isn't it clean enough?"

Javi shrugged, and Foster led the way to the house. "You can wash up in there," he said, leading the way to the back sink and then

33

washing his hands. The house smelled of eggs, bacon, and cinnamon. He hoped his grandmother had been baking her rolls. It sure smelled like it. "I love you," he told Grandma Katie when he saw the pan sitting on the stove to cool.

"You're just in time," she said and turned to Javi. "But this one is rarely late for food. I swear, he could be out on the far side of the farm and yet hear the timer go off if I have something in the oven."

Javi laughed, deep and rich, without self-consciousness. It was a warm and full sound, sending another jolt through Foster, who pointed Javi to a chair and then took one himself. He was tempted to sit at the opposite side of the table, but that would be rude, so he sat next to Javi and waited for his mother to join them. She came in dressed in rough clothes to work outside and took her place at the foot of the table, where she always sat. Foster jumped up and brought the dishes to the table while his grandmother dished up the cinnamon rolls that already had his mouth watering.

"I used to have to limit Foster to one or he'd eat the entire pan at a sitting," his mother said, and Foster groaned. *What is this, Tell Foster Stories Day?*

"I'd still eat the entire pan, but I'm more generous now." He bumped Javi's shoulder and then wondered if he was being too forward and familiar.

Grandma Katie sat down, and they all ate. Foster was hungry, but it was obvious Javi was starving. His eyes glazed over, and he made a deep, happy sound in his throat as he ate. If Foster had eaten that quickly, his mother and grandmother would have scolded him, but no one said a word, and once Javi's plate was empty, Foster's mother added more food.

Foster shared glances with his mother and grandmother, silently wondering if they were going to ask the questions they all seemed to want to. Of course, no one did, and Javi appeared oblivious as he ate his fill.

"I'll clean up," his mother volunteered, so Foster and Grandma Katie led Javi out to the garden.

"We enlarged it this year, but that means that this section is really prone to weeds, as you can see already. We have to be careful not to pull any sprouting plants." Foster settled Javi in Grandma Katie's strawberry patch, which was growing like crazy. "Get the large weeds. The smaller ones will get choked out by the strawberries."

"Okay," Javi said, and they settled down to work while Foster's grandmother got to the more detailed work. "Shouldn't she be doing the easier work?"

"Please," Grandma Katie snapped from where she sat on a low stool, picking the weeds from the sprouts. "I've been pulling weeds since before your daddy was born."

Foster grinned and looked away to keep from scoffing. "Never tell her she can't do something." He'd pulled more than his fair share of weeds, but Javi was a machine. His hands were nimble and efficient as he emptied a section of the patch and started on another. The plants were loaded with berries; even the ones that had been planted the year before were robust and thick.

"I guess not," Javi said, sounding as though he wasn't sure how seriously to take her. Foster smiled at him, and Javi relaxed a little. "Do you sell to people around here?"

"You mean to other farmers?"

"Sure. You're on a corner." Javi sat on his haunches. "You could put up a small stand right over there and sell things. You could see when people stopped from the house or just put out a box for them to leave the money in." Javi grew quiet and went back to pulling weeds. "Don't listen to me. I shouldn't have said anything."

"No. It's a good idea. No one else in this area has these berries or our asparagus. We could sell some of those when the time comes." He turned to his grandmother. "Maybe we could sell preserves and things too. Everyone loves them. We'd need to develop labels with the ingredients, but we could print those easily enough." Foster looked over at Javi, who was trying not to smile. "I like the idea."

"You'd have to build something," Javi offered.

"Maybe not. We could buy a building that isn't too large and customize it." Foster began thinking out loud. "If the venture doesn't work, we could move the building and put it to use for something else." The idea was already taking root in his mind. They needed to increase cash flow, and they had some unique products they could use to do it.

"Raspberries," Grandma Katie said. "We should plant some."

"But they're prickly and hard to grow well." Not to mention invasive. They'd had some years ago and they'd ended up being removed.

"I read about a couple varieties. They grow up, and then you cut them to the ground after harvesting every year. You don't need the year-old cane to produce fruit. They also aren't prickly. Check on the Internet." She went back to her work, and Foster's mother came out and joined her.

The sun was strong and the heat built. Foster didn't want his mother and grandmother out in the heat of the day, so the women went inside just before noon, having made good progress, and Foster and Javi finished up.

"Is there anything else you need me to do?" Javi asked.

"I need to check the fields I planted a few weeks ago. How does the asparagus look?"

"Monday should be right on target. They're starting to sprout and should have some good stalks, at least enough to make it worth cutting."

"Excellent," Foster said, and Javi looked at him strangely. "What's that look for?"

"Nothing," Javi said as he schooled his expression.

"You don't get off that easily." He watched and waited.

"You believe me. Just like that."

Foster mimicked Javi's earlier expression. "Why wouldn't I?"

Javi shrugged and began gathering the tools. Having a meaningful conversation with him was like pulling teeth.

"Just explain what you meant," Foster said.

"No one listens to me or asks my opinion." Javi carried the tools toward the shed, and Foster got the rest. "My dad rules the family, and what he says goes. So even though I knew it was a bad idea, he had one too many beers and argued with the boss at our last job, demanding more money. He said we'd go on strike, so the boss sent us packing. We ran out of food a day before getting here, and the van was running on fumes. He sent me up to see if you had work for me, and when I got home, he took the money I earned." Javi ground his teeth, the heat in his eyes enough to scorch the grass. "I tried to tell him...."

Foster thought of his own relationship with his father. "Sometimes fathers think they know best and get used to being the boss. I stood up to mine... but that might not work with your dad." With his, respect had been the issue. Foster got the idea that with Javi's father, it was about power and control. Two very different concerns.

Javi put the tools in the shed, and Foster added his own before closing the door. "My dad had beer on his breath when he came in last night."

"Where did he get it?"

"He left us under the awning while he took the van to get food. He returned with some, but he'd also been drinking." The resentment was clear in Javi's voice. He'd been the one to earn the money, and for his father to be that selfish....

People often surprised Foster. He liked to see the best in people and to think that they were basically good. Mothers and fathers, in his view, should put their children and family first. "I'll pay you some of what you earned today, and the rest I can hold so you can have it later." If what Javi said was true, then he was the one who really cared and would make sure everyone ate. "If that's what you want," he added at Javi's unreadable expression.

"It won't do any good," Javi said with resignation, rubbing the back of his neck nervously. "I can't hide money or anything from him. We all live in a space that's as big as the inside of your shed. There isn't any room for secrets."

"All right. Whatever you think is best." Foster wanted to help Javi, not come between him and his parents. He led the way to the truck and motioned to Javi to follow him. Foster had forgotten, in just a few weeks, that work went better and was less like drudgery when he had someone along with him. "Let's fill the back with silage, and we can spread it for the herd to give some of the grass a break." After the rain, he wanted to be careful that the cows didn't chew up the soft earth, so he'd left them in an enclosed area near the barn.

He parked the truck at the silo, and they began filling the back. Javi once again went quiet as he worked. The task didn't take long, and Foster drove the truck as close to the feeding station as possible. He should have made sure the feeders were totally full before letting the cattle into the area. But the feeders were close enough to the fence that they were able to easily fill them.

His arms ached by the time they were done, and he cursed himself for not thinking far enough ahead. He should have filled the feeders before putting the herd in the pasture. The herd didn't care—they were already eating—but he felt completely stupid. His father would have reminded him not to put the herd in there, but he hadn't been thinking at the time. Foster said nothing, dropping the pitchfork into the truck bed and sitting on the side.

"What's the rest of your family doing while you're here?" he asked Javi.

"Mom is with the kids, and Dad is working at a farm out the other way." He pointed down the road. "He's working with horses. Can I ask what you do with all the mess? The cow poop."

"Some I spread on the fields as fertilizer. But I have to be careful when I spread it in order to ensure it breaks down enough before harvest. I have a company that takes it away to make fuel out of it. There's a plant not too far away that will take it. They make gas out of it that they can sell or burn to make electricity." That reminded him: he needed to call and have a load picked up. There was always something.

"My mom said your dad died. I'm sorry."

Foster picked at some dirt on the truck. "I'm still trying to remember to do all the things he used to do." What Foster was realizing was that he needed some help, but he wasn't sure how he'd be able to afford it. Having Javi work with him for a few days was nice, but he needed someone he could rely on to do a regular part of the work so he could manage the business.

"You'll figure it all out," Javi said, sitting across from him.

"I'm not so sure. It's only been a few weeks, and I've got all these things I want to try, but sometimes I can barely keep my head on the tasks that I have to do."

Javi shrugged. "When I'm working, I do one thing, make sure it's done, and then move on."

"I know about that. But I'm supposed to do the chores, sell what the farm produces, plan how to make the business more successful, and somehow keep from working my mother and grandmother to death." Yeah, he was feeling sorry for himself, and that had to stop. It was counterproductive.

"At least you have a place to live," Javi said, looking around. Foster stared at him. "I haven't ever lived in a house like you have. My family has moved from place to place with the crops for as long as I can remember. Sometimes we stay in the van, like we are here. Five people in a van. Other times there's quarters that the farmer lets us use. The last one had a dirt floor and was overrun with termites and scorpions."

Foster nodded, knowing he had very little to complain about, really. "You're right." It put a lot of things in perspective. "Let's go check the fields, and then we can have lunch." There was always more work to be done. "How are you with tools? Building things."

"I've done just about anything I've ever been asked."

The equipment shed needed some repairs, and it would be much easier with some help. They got in the truck, and Foster pulled away and down the drive. He turned right and took the road toward the back of the property. He pulled to a stop at the edge of the first field. He got out, looking across the largely flat area that was just greening up, the corn spreading its first leaves. He checked that soil, rolling it between his fingers. The soil in their area could have a sandy consistency, but Foster and his family had been blessed with just a small amount of clay, and that helped hold the moisture rather than letting it wick away.

"Is it okay?" Javi asked.

"Yes. Everything is growing." And the weeds hadn't had a chance to get much of a start. It wouldn't be long before the corn took all the sun and made it impossible for weeds to have a chance except at the edges of the field. "I hate using a lot of pesticides and chemicals. They end up in the cows and then in the milk." Quality was their stock-in-trade, and he didn't want to jeopardize that. "Let's move on."

They got back in the truck and went from field to field, with good results. It seemed that the hours he'd spent in the tractor planting were going to pay off. But he had to caution himself that it was still early in the growing season and there was a lot that could happen. He wondered if Javi wanted to check in with his family, but he said nothing, so Foster drove back to the farm. They went right inside for lunch. His mother had made sandwiches. It was an easy lunch, but Javi didn't seem to mind, judging by the way he ate. Foster didn't want to pry.

His mother had no such compunctions. "Do you always eat that much?"

"No, ma'am," Javi answered, clearly embarrassed judging by the red that colored his otherwise bronze cheeks.

"I like a man who eats. Tells me that the food is good." She gave Foster one of those looks and then shifted her gaze to Javi.

Foster rolled his eyes and thought that his mother might have made a nice save. Then she passed Javi the plate. What began bothering Foster was that if Javi was hungry, what about the rest of the family? Yes, he and Javi had done a lot of hard work and that brought on an appetite, but he didn't think that accounted for the amount Javi was eating. Javi had told him things had been rough for his family, but Foster wondered if there was more going on that Javi hadn't shared or wasn't privy to.

"I should get the supplies together," Foster said once he was finished and pushed away from the table.

"What are you doing?" his mother asked.

Giving you the few minutes with Javi you seem to want. "Dad got asphalt shingles a few weeks ago, and we were going to fix the toolshed roof...." He didn't need to continue and upset his mother. "Finish your lunch and join me in the yard," he added to Javi and left the kitchen.

The sun was strong and hot. June could be a fickle month. Sometimes, if the wind was strong off the lake, it could be wet and cool. This year had been sunny and warm so far, but Foster knew to take advantage when the weather was good because that could change fast.

He found the shingles in the shed, so he got them out and stacked them to the side of the door. He'd thought about putting the new roof over the old but was concerned about the weight, especially mixed with snow in the winter, so he got a ladder and began tearing off the old roof. He was well into it when Javi climbed up to join him and they each took a side.

"I always hate jobs like this," Foster confessed.

"Why?" Javi dropped a load of shingles to the ground and then went back down the ladder. Foster peered over the side, watching as Javi brought a wheelbarrow to his side of the roof and then parked another on the other side.

"Good idea." The shed wasn't that large, but the cleanup of all the old shingles was going to be a mess. Javi climbed back on the roof, and they finished clearing it off, filling the wheelbarrows and then dumping them in the trash containers. The wheelbarrows filled quickly, and it took a while to rake up the old nails, which they had to be pretty careful about.

"Have you roofed before?" Foster asked.

"Not really. I'll haul up the shingles so you can get started." Javi tugged off his shirt, shoving it into his back pocket before hoisting a bag on his shoulder and slowly climbing the ladder. Foster got the nail gun and compressor before climbing up himself. He set the first row of shingles, making sure they were straight. He wasn't nearly as proficient as the guys who did this all the time, but it didn't take him long to get into a rhythm. It was a simple, two-sided, pitched roof, so there was little cutting, and that could mostly be done at the end. He took off his shirt, dropped it to the ground, and settled in to work.

Javi reached the top of the ladder and set down another bundle of shingles.

"Dammit." Foster needed to be careful. He had let his attention wander and nearly nailed his hand, yanking it back just before the nail gun got it. He needed to be paying attention to his work instead of the smooth copper skin and perfect small nipples that stuck out just right from the planes of Javi's chest. Foster knew he shouldn't be looking at the lines on Javi's belly or the trail of dark, wispy hair that started at his belly button and disappeared into the top of his thin jeans.

He lowered his gaze, trying not to make too big a deal of it, and grabbed the next sheet of shingles. He placed them, put in the nails, and reached for the next sheet. He thought Javi had descended and chanced a look. This time he saw Javi look at him and then turn away before climbing down the ladder.

A fluttery warmth started in Foster's belly, spreading though his legs and up his arms, settling at the base of his brain like the buzzing of a bee. He was glad to have a second to adjust his dick because it was hard, aching, and he didn't want to be obvious. The last thing he wanted was for Javi to go running back to his family thinking Foster had been perving on him. Granted, the thoughts Foster was having were most definitely pervy and involved finding out if Javi's skin was as soft and his muscles as hard as they looked.

He set the sheet of shingles and continued, placing sheet after sheet, row after row until he approached the peak of the roof. Then he switched sides and heard Javi shifting the ladder. He set the first row the same way he'd done the other side. Foster turned as a rip of fabric sounded and the back of his leg suddenly felt breezy. Damn nail.

"God," Foster said as he put the gun on the roof and it slid down toward the edge. He caught it, but that meant pulling his hand away from his backside, and he was once again flashing his butt at Javi. "I think I need to go change my pants."

Javi got on the roof, and Foster made his way down and over to the house. He went right up to his room and kicked off his shoes.

Once he got his pants off, he was surprised to see the seam of his Levi's had given way, tearing up the leg and over the seat. Foster tried to remember how long he'd had them and couldn't. He usually wore older clothes when he was doing heavy work. After putting them aside so his mom or grandmother could see if they could be repaired, he pulled on another pair and put his shoes back on, then hurried back out to the shed.

Thankfully there were no further wardrobe malfunctions that afternoon, but Foster was distracted off and on by Javi and the way the sun shone off his lightly sweat-sheened shoulders and chest. Part of him reveled in the wonder of curiosity. His body tingled in a way that was foreign to him, and he wanted to get closer to Javi, while at the same time, he needed to finish the roof before he did something he'd regret.

The afternoon was turning to evening by the time they finished the ridge and climbed down the ladder for the last time. Javi began cleaning up the mess around the shed while Foster put away the tools. He set the nail gun on the shelf in the shed under the roof they'd just completed, held the edge of the bench, and sighed, closing his eyes. All he saw was Javi—skin shining in the sun, sometimes watching him when he thought Foster wasn't looking. At least he thought Javi had been watching him. But what if he hadn't been, and the interest or curiosity—whatever he wanted to call it—had all been in Foster's imagination? Foster might not have had much experience with running the farm on his own, but he knew he shouldn't be having feelings for someone who worked for him, let alone another guy.

"Are we done for the day?" Javi asked after he gathered up the last of the wrappers from the shingles and spent some time raking the area around the shed once again.

Foster kept his distance. He figured that was best, so he busied himself inside, putting away the remaining shingles and cleaning up. "Yes. Let me pay you."

"Do you need me tomorrow?"

"It's supposed to rain," Foster said instead of giving him a straightforward answer. It was probably good that he spend some time away from him. Maybe he could clear his mind and get this… fascination with Javi out of his system.

"What if it's nice?" Javi asked.

"Then come down," he answered before he could stop himself. He did his best not to stare at Javi's chest and the way his jeans now hung low on his hips and the lines on his belly pointed toward hidden treasures. Foster licked his lips in order to get some moisture in his suddenly dry mouth.

"Javi," Foster's mother called as she hurried over. "The shed looks good, boys." She smiled and faced Javi. "I made a casserole. It's baked pasta with meat sauce. Come inside when you're ready to go, and you can take it with you." It looked like Javi might protest, but Foster knew his mother's expression and that she wouldn't take no for an answer.

"Thank you," Javi said. He grabbed his shirt and shrugged it on. "I was about to walk home."

"I'll take you," his mother said, and Foster watched as she led him inside the house. Breathing a sigh of relief, he went into the barn, used the sink to wash up, and then let in the herd to begin the milking process.

FOSTER WAS a mess. He'd finished the milking and eaten his dinner. Now he was trying to do some work in the office, but he wasn't getting anywhere.

"You know you don't have to do it all," his mother said from the doorway. She came in and sat down in a chair. "I used to do the books for your father when we were first married. But after you were born, I was busy and the house chores got heavier, so we transitioned it away."

"Why didn't you say so?" Foster complained.

"It's been a long time, and back then I did everything on paper and in ledgers. Your dad used the computer, and I let him take care of it. He always said it didn't take very long."

"Then maybe we can do this together." He needed help and he wasn't ashamed to say so. "I'm getting overwhelmed, but I'm afraid that I can't afford to hire some help."

She pulled the chair up to the desk, and he turned the screen so she could see it. Then they began.

After two hours Foster was about ready to collapse, but his mother was a barrel of energy. He'd shown her how the systems worked, and she'd been able to bring order and context to some of what had seemed like chaos to him.

"The tools have changed, but what I knew still applies," she said.

"Yes, it does." He slid back and stood, letting her take control of the computer. Foster sat in the second chair and leaned back. He rested his head, and when it fell forward, he jerked awake. His mother was still staring at the screen and going through invoices.

"Our expenses are fairly minimal and have been for a number of years. The equipment we have is paid for. It's older but ours. We grow a lot of our own feed, and what we don't we trade for." She continued looking and working.

"It's the price of the milk that's killing us. We aren't getting much for it. Not based on what milk costs in the stores," Foster told her. It had been the perpetual debate and grouse in the family.

"Is that why you were talking about cheese?" she asked him.

"Yeah. If we can add value, we can get more for the dairy products. But that's a large investment of time and money." Especially if his grandmother was the one with the knowledge. Not that she couldn't show them how to make the cheese, but he and his mother already had plenty to do.

"We can look into it in the future. We're expanding into the farmer's markets as well as a stand here, so let's see how that goes." She pushed back from the desk. "We're making money on the dairy operation, but not enough to keep the farm going and pay us something for our efforts. It keeps the lights on, but that's all at these prices."

"No wonder Dad was borrowing money," Foster said as he stood up. "I've got so many ideas, Mom. I'd like to expand the dairy herd and be able to make our own cheeses, really special things. Our herd is from great bloodlines. We could let it grow naturally for a few years and then build a side business in calves. I want to buy additional land to use to grow even more vegetables, like boutique potatoes, garlic, and other types of greens and squash. That way we could have vegetables for the stand and market year-round."

"Hold on, honey," she said with a smile.

"I know we can't do all that at once, but I want to be able to actually make the farm really pay so you and Grandma don't have to work so hard. Mr. Dulles said that we have to treat the farm as a business, and that struck a chord with me."

"Okay. Let's take it one step at a time." She stood. "But don't you dare think about keeping chickens. I hate those things, and I will not gather any damned eggs."

Foster had no intention of adding chickens to the mix.

"I'm going to go to bed." His mother yawned. "I still have a hard time sleeping, and I probably will for a long time."

Foster nodded slowly. "I miss him too." He hugged his mother tightly and felt her start to cry. Tears welled in his eyes as well. His father hadn't been an easy man to get to know or get along with, but he had been there for him. He'd milked cows and then helped Foster build Pinewood Derby cars for Scouts, even when he was so tired he couldn't think straight. He'd helped Foster with 4-H projects, and the blue, white, and red ribbons were still in a box under Foster's bed. He'd delighted in those ribbons, but they had been his father's just as much as they'd been his. "How am I going to run this place without him?"

She hugged him closer. "Just follow your heart. It's what I'm trying to do." She let him go, and Foster wiped his eyes. "I need to go up to bed," she said. He reached for the box of tissues and she took one and dabbed her eyes with it. "I keep wishing I'd insisted he go to the doctor. I should have shoved the stubborn old goat into the car and driven him there myself." She looked toward the ceiling, muttering under her breath. "God help me, I love him, but your father was one pigheaded mule."

Foster didn't argue. "I'll be up soon."

She nodded and left the room.

Foster turned out the lights and went out back, doing a last check of the herd and making sure all the barn doors were closed before returning to the dark, silent house and going up to bed. He undressed, cleaned up, and got into bed. He was so tired his eyes closed on their own, but his head had different ideas.

He thought about his father and the work he had to do. That sent his mind careening down the path of the work they'd done today, and of course he ended up playing images of Javi in his head. Fuck, it was difficult to sleep with a hard-on. He ran his hands down his chest and then between his legs, stroking his cock slowly, twisting his hand around the head just the way he liked it.

He let himself sink into his fantasy, watching as Javi stood shirtless on the roof. Thankfully fantasies were never rational, because Javi started doing a striptease right there on the roof, those thin pants sliding down his legs. Damn, Javi was fine-looking, and suddenly they'd changed locations and Javi was in his room with him, sliding work-roughened hands down Foster's naked belly, wrapping callused fingers around his cock, scratching just enough to make it feel so good and....

Foster held his breath, warmth spreading through him, and then he was coming, doing his best not to make too much noise so no one would know what he'd been doing. He breathed as steadily as he could, head swimming in a sea of endorphins. He reached for a tissue from the box beside the bed and held still, lying where he was and letting the happiness linger. Of course it never lasted long enough.

He wiped himself up and then threw away the evidence of his fun before rolling onto his side away from the open windows and closing his eyes. Usually once he had a fantasy and the fireworks were over, it all faded away, but not tonight. Javi stayed in his mind, on the edges of his thoughts. He listened to the crickets and lowing of the herd outside his window, carried on the wind. But after a while he also heard the sounds, in his mind, anyway, of Javi climbing up and down that ladder, the squeak, the slight grunt when he lifted the package on his shoulder. And no matter what he did to stop it or how much he tried to put the image out of his head, he kept seeing Javi, shirt off, glistening in the sun.

CHAPTER 4

THERE WAS still a morning chill in the air as Foster shuffled into the barn with his mug of coffee. He was way too dang tired today. He finished the hot liquid and rinsed the mug out, setting it next to the sink before staring down the empty milking floor. He usually loved this time of the morning. The sun was just peeking over the horizon, and the day held nothing but promise. But Foster couldn't help wondering what was going to happen. He had the feeling something important was just around the corner. Of course, that usually meant things were about to go to hell in a handbasket, as his grandmother said sometimes.

Now that his coffee had begun to work, Foster began letting the herd into the barn and into the milking stalls. Once they were set, he started the process.

"Are you in here?" Javi called, and Foster looked up from where he was installing the milker.

"Give me a few minutes." He moved on to the next one. "I need to get this process finished."

"I can start in the garden," Javi offered, and Foster agreed. The best way to get the milking done was to keep up his rhythm. He finished the first set of cows, turned them out into the pasture, and brought in the next, got them milked and then turned out once again. After the milking was done, he cleaned the area, hosing down everything, and then washed his hands. A few minutes later the familiar *beep beep* of a truck backing up sounded, and Foster got ready for the dairy to take delivery of the milk.

He talked with the driver for a few minutes and verified that all the records were correct. Then he washed out the empty holding tanks so they would be ready for the fresh milk that night.

"The garden is pretty clear of weeds," Javi told him from the doorway.

"Great." He did a mental checklist in his head. The herd was in one of the pastures, where they'd spend the day. They had feed and were in good shape. Though he did make a note to look for some of the cows after milking and separate them for calving.

"You work hard," Javi said, looking around. "Everything is so clean. You'd hardly know this was a barn."

"We don't want anything to get into the milk, so everything from the cows, to the udders, the barn, and the milk room has to be kept as clean as possible. We disinfect the surfaces in here and keep the tanks and all of the milk systems super clean. The dairy tests the milk when they pick it up to ensure it's as pure as possible. I think dairy farming is in my blood. Sometimes when I cut myself, I expect to bleed milk."

"What do we need to do today?"

"Clean," Foster said. He went to the mudroom area and got an extra pair of boots. "See if these fit." He felt a slight twinge of guilt since those were his father's boots. He had at first looked for an extra pair of his, but his father's looked like they might fit, and they were only boots. Still, he felt a little sad about it. Just another way his father was getting farther away from him.

Once Javi was ready, Foster explained how to hose down everything. "I did a good cleanup after the herd left, but I want to make sure there isn't anything hiding anywhere."

"So this is extra?"

"Yeah." He turned on the hose and began in one of the corners, instructing Javi to do the same. "I see this every day, and I try to be as clean as humanly possible, but sometimes you need to look at things differently."

Javi pointed to a spot up on the wall and aimed his hose at it. "How did that get there?"

"Sometimes cow crap goes everywhere," Foster said. It was his only explanation, since the cows were pointed away from the walls. He returned to work, and five minutes later a spray of water hit him square in the back, soaking his shirt, sending water running down into his pants.

"Sorry," Javi called. "It got away from me a little."

"I bet it did," Foster retorted and went back to work. He found a few places that he'd missed and made sure they were clean. To a lot of people it seemed dumb to clean where cows were going to make a mess, but it all went into ensuring that the farm's product remained as good quality as possible.

"Hey!" Foster cried when Javi got him again with the water. He continued working and then shot water at Javi a minute later.

"That's cold," Javi said. "At least I didn't do it on purpose."

Foster giggled like an idiot. He was wet and cold himself, but watching Javi dance as the water ran down his back and into his pants was precious. Of course, that lasted about two seconds before Foster realized Javi's jeans were now hugging his perfect bubble-shaped backside. He turned away and got more water for his trouble.

"So that's how it is," Foster growled and shot Javi with more water. The hose fight was on. Foster dodged Javi's spray and caught him dead center in the chest. Javi returned fire as Foster raced to the controls and turned off Javi's hose.

"Not fair," he groused as the water dried up.

Foster lifted his hose, pointing the nozzle at Javi as he hurried closer, fully intent on soaking him.

Then he stopped. Javi's shirt clung to his chest, his nipples perked up, denting the fabric outward. As cold and wet as Foster was from the water, the sight still caused a rush of heat to wash through him.

Javi licked his lips, and Foster forgot about the hose in his hand or getting Javi any wetter. He let the nozzle slip from his fingers and took a step closer. Part of him said this was wrong, but that little voice was overpowered by the heat racing through his veins and the pounding in his chest. His belly was doing excited flip-flops, and when Javi took a single step closer and then stilled, Foster hoped like hell he wasn't reading this wrong.

"I should be cold," Javi whispered.

"Me too." Foster watched Javi's lips and then locked gazes with him. What he saw was heat glowing back at him. At least he hoped to high heaven that's what it was. "Is this…. Am I wrong…?" He wasn't sure how to ask what he wanted to know. He didn't have words that wouldn't sound crass or stupid, and he wanted neither of those at the moment.

"I shouldn't…," Javi began, even as he took another step closer. Foster closed the gap between them and stopped. For the first time, he slid his hand along Javi's jaw, caressing stubbly warmth. He had no idea what he was doing. The only model he had for a situation like this was the love scenes he'd seen in movies or on television, and they certainly hadn't prepared him for what to do with Javi. But he did draw Javi closer and kiss him.

He hadn't been sure what to expect when he kissed another guy. He'd kissed a few girls and nothing had happened. Their lips had been nice and all, but there was no energy. With Javi there was plenty of that. Foster pulled away, watching Javi blink, and heard him gasp slightly.

"Is it always like that?" Javi asked, and Foster shrugged.

"Maybe because it's my first time…. You know, with a guy," Foster whispered. He was just as blind as Javi seemed to be. "It wasn't like this with the few girls I've kissed."

"Same here." Javi shuddered, and Foster smiled.

"Not very good?" he asked, and Javi shook his head. "Me either." He leaned forward, kissing Javi once again.

"Fos-ter." His mother's call drifted through the barn. They shifted apart and Javi blushed, turning to pick up his hose. Foster turned the water back on as he went to see what his mother wanted.

Foster tromped to the doorway. "Yeah, Mom," he said over his heart pounding in his ears.

"Is everything okay?"

"It's fine. We're doing some extra cleaning, and then we'll be done for the morning. I'm going to take Javi back and check that we can cut on Monday." He didn't want his mother to see him dripping all over the place. At least talking to her had sent his throbbing cock back to normal. He figured nothing did that for any guy like talking to his mother.

"Is there anything you need from town? Your grandmother needs to get some things from the drugstore, and I'm going grocery shopping."

"Nope. I'm fine. Thanks." He went back into the barn. Javi was hard at work and didn't turn around when he approached. Foster watched him for a few seconds, hoping he'd acknowledge him. Then Foster picked up his hose and got back to work as well. They washed down everything for the next half hour, with no more water fights and hardly a word unless Javi had a question about some stain.

Everything in the milking barn dripped by the time they were done, but it was spick-and-span clean. Foster turned off the water and began gathering up the hoses, watching Javi. "I'm sorry if I…." What the hell did he say at a time like this? Maybe it would be best if he let it go and didn't talk about it again.

"No. I…."

Foster set the hoses on their holders, stepped out into the mudroom, and began pulling off his boots. His feet and socks were soaked, as were most of his clothes. "I should have kept to myself. I didn't mean to make you feel bad."

Javi tugged off the boots and took off his socks, which were full of holes. He set them aside and put his bare feet back into his old sneakers. "If my family found out I was… like this… they'd never speak to me again."

Foster nodded. He didn't know how his own family would react.

"We have a name for people like me, and it isn't very nice." Javi pulled his shirt away from his body.

"I know those words. I've heard the English versions enough in my life. Not used against me, but I've heard them." Foster pulled on his shoes. "Come on. Let's go in the house. I think I can find you something dry to wear." He looked Javi up and down as if sizing him up, but all he was doing was taking in his tall, broad frame. The man was stunningly gorgeous, not too bulky, but strong and lean with eyes that Foster couldn't seem to turn away from.

"I think you can stop that," Javi said, stuttering slightly, and then he smiled.

"Sorry."

"I've always been told that this is wrong. I know the court said that guys like us could get married and all, but they never said that your family couldn't throw you out or never talk to you again."

"Do you think that could happen, just from a kiss?"

"No. I think it could happen because I want to do more than kiss." Javi sighed. Foster did the same, and they walked out of the barn and across the yard. "Where is everyone?"

"They went into town," Foster answered as he pulled open the back door and led the way inside. They took off their shoes, and Foster led the way through the house and up to his room. He closed the door and rummaged in his closet. Javi was a little taller than he was, and broader. He found a Michigan T-shirt his mother had bought for him that was a size too big. That was the easy part. Pants would be harder, but he found some gray track pants and handed them over to Javi as well. "The bathroom is right there," he said, pointing.

Javi nodded and pulled his shirt over his head. Foster watched, riveted on each new inch of exposed flesh. How could he not look when Javi was giving him a show he wasn't expecting? When the first button on his jeans opened, Foster swallowed. At the second button, his mouth went dry as he dared to hope that Javi was going to finish changing right there. By the third, his breath hitched in his throat, and when Javi let go of the wet material and stepped out of the jeans, Foster wasn't sure if he was going to pass out or not.

"Jesus." To say Javi was breathtaking was an understatement. He was hard, his long, thick cock pointing toward the ceiling, foreskin pulled back until the entire head was exposed. "I thought you were worried about—"

Javi cut off what Foster was going to say by kissing his breath away.

Foster's knees shook and for a second he wasn't sure what he should do. So many late nights he'd wondered and dreamed what it would be like to have a man, naked, with him, close enough to touch, and he was shocked into stillness.

"Is this bad?" Javi asked.

The confusion in his voice pulled Foster out of his bewilderment. "No," he breathed as he pulled his wet shirt over his head.

"Good. I thought I might be doing something wrong. Maybe I'm not a good kisser." Javi chuckled. "I heard my mom say once that my father kissed like a largemouth bass. She was talking to one of her lady friends at one of the camps when we were down south."

"You're a good kisser, with nothing in common with a fish," Foster said. "I've just never done anything like this." He got his socks off and then undid his jeans. "I'm not sure what to do."

Javi scoffed lightly. "You live on a farm—there has to be plenty of nature doing what nature does."

Foster shoved down his pants and kicked them off to stand naked in front of Javi. "This is a dairy farm. There's nothing about procreation here that's natural. The bull stuff comes in a vat, and the most romantic thing they get is what the vet uses." God, he couldn't believe he was talking about this when he and Javi were naked and they only had so much time before his mother came home. Foster pulled Javi to him, guiding them to the bed and then down onto the mattress. His heart raced as Javi rolled him on the mattress, pressing down onto him.

That was fine with Foster, because it gave him free rein with his hands, and he used them to explore Javi's strong back, running his finger along a slight ridge he found running across the base of his back. "What's this?"

Javi stilled, his gaze meeting Foster's. "My dad drank too much a few years ago and got mad at me. That's the scar from his belt."

Foster pulled his hands away and brought them to Javi's cheeks. "I'm sorry. I…." Hell, what should he say? He was sorry Javi's father was a douche bag? He brought Javi's head down, their lips found their counterpart, and Foster concentrated on the energy that zinged between them. This was like a drug that he could definitely get addicted to.

Javi began grinding his hips slowly, and Foster moaned as his cock slid on Javi's belly. He closed his eyes, kissed Javi again, and let his head swim with the new sensation. He'd stroked himself off plenty over the years, but this wasn't like that. His hand on his dick was one thing, but Javi's skin was something completely different.

"Wow," Foster whispered. "That's really nice. How did you know to do that?"

"Just doing what feels good," Javi answered, moving more forcefully.

"I like that feeling." Foster wound his hands around to Javi's butt. Damn, it was hard and firm, flexing as he moved. Foster tightened his hold and thrust upward. Damn, that was wonderful.

"Me too." Javi's voice shook as the rest of him began to quiver. "I… damn…."

"Uh-huh," he whispered, throwing his head back as his cock grew even more sensitive. He held Javi tighter, kissed him hard, and then lost himself in the swirl of his intense dark eyes. Within seconds they deepened further as heat spread between them. "Oh man," Foster whispered, forgetting himself for a few seconds.

"Is… something… wrong?" Javi gasped.

Foster held him tight as he stilled. "No. It was right. Your eyes were so incredible, and the way you held your lips apart and the muscles of your cheek quivered as you came. It was pretty amazing." He'd come lots of times, but seeing another guy climax was pretty damned awesome.

"What about you?" Javi asked, and Foster tried to roll them on the bed, but the look of panic in Javi's eyes stopped him cold. He thrust upward, holding Javi's asscheeks, and sank into the depth of his amazing brown eyes. Javi's reaction confused him, but he was too close and seconds from being too far gone to think about it now. His leg shook and his hands quivered as heat began at the base of his balls, radiating out through him. The tingling started right afterward, and between them they were too much for him to contain. Foster groaned and clamped his eyes closed as the pressure built, becoming greater, more than he could control, and within seconds he came, lights flashing behind his eyes. Then warmth took over, and he floated on his release while Javi held him bound to the earth.

It was fantastic being held in Javi's arms. Neither of them moved for a while, not that Foster wanted to. He was completely content right where he was. "That was… wow."

"You can say that again," Javi mumbled and then grew quiet. "I should get dressed and go back to my family. They will be wondering about me."

That seemed like such a strange thing to say. Foster lifted his gaze so he could look into Javi's eyes. But he got nothing other than swirling confusion and worry. Javi bit his lower lip, and Foster kissed him, trying to reassure him but not knowing how. "They know where you are."

Javi nodded but offered no further explanation for his concern. Foster slowly got up and went to the bathroom, where he wiped his belly and grabbed a towel. He handed it to Javi, watching him, wondering what he should do next. It seemed rude to just get dressed, but he wasn't sure what Javi wanted him to do. Foster would have been content to climb back into the bed, lie next to Javi, and close his eyes for some much-needed rest. For a farmer that was the ultimate decadence, resting during the day.

Once Javi wiped his belly, he handed Foster back the towel and sat up, legs dangling over the edge of the mattress, running his hands worriedly through his hair. "I'm in real trouble."

"Did we do… did I do something wrong?"

Javi lifted his gaze from the floor. "Yes… no.…"

Foster blinked, hoping for some explanation for the confusion.

"I mean, it was nice and you didn't do anything wrong, not when we were together, but maybe we did something wrong."

Foster sighed. "This is so confusing. I liked being with you. It was… special." He sat down next to Javi. "I mean, it was hot and all, but it also felt special."

"I know. But this is wrong."

"Is that what people told you?" He knew what he'd been told at church and stuff, but he didn't always believe what the minister said. But he thought his mother did and believed his father had as well.

"Of course."

"Well…." Foster sighed and scratched the back of his head. "Maybe we should stop listening to what others say and think for ourselves." He turned toward Javi, pulling his leg up on the bed. "People used to say that the world was flat. Did that make the world flat? No. It just made the people who thought so wrong." Foster shrugged. "So people say being gay is wrong. So what? Maybe that's like the flat-world thing."

"Yeah, but…."

"Do you want to be with girls?" Foster asked, and Javi shook his head. "Do you want to get married and spend the rest of your life with a woman?" Javi paled and shook his head one more time. "I didn't choose to be gay. Did you?"

Javi smiled. "No."

"Then maybe being gay is right for us. I'm no expert, and I wish I knew someone I could ask, but I don't."

Javi gasped. "You'd talk to someone about this? About us and what we did?" He sounded as though that was the most foreign thing in the world.

"If I thought they could help. Don't you have like a million questions that you'd like answered? I know I do." Foster got off the bed and went to the window. The yard was quiet. "I thought I heard something."

Javi stood and began pulling on the dry clothes Foster had given him. "Maybe your mom will be back soon, and…." He raked his gaze over Foster, who felt the heat of it sliding up his legs and then over his belly and chest. "I need some time to think about this."

"I don't have any answers. I wish I did." Foster stepped closer to Javi. "But there is one thing I know." He cupped Javi's cheeks in his hands and drew their lips together, kissing him hard, demanding, his body instantly reacting to Javi's closeness. When Javi responded, placing his hands on Foster's hips and then sliding them down to his ass, Foster was ready to go again. Heat surged through him, and he was already pressing Javi toward the bed before he could think about it. "I want…," Foster mumbled, and when Javi sat down, Foster pressed him back, working his hand into Javi's borrowed track pants. He pulled them down, freeing Javi's cock, and stared at it before opening his mouth and sucking the glistening head between his lips.

"Oh God," Javi groaned, falling back on the bed, stretching out like a cat in the sun.

Salt, sweet, and musk burst on his tongue. At first Foster wasn't sure he liked it, but it was Javi, the taste of him, and as he sucked harder and Javi moaned softly, he couldn't get enough. Foster bobbed his head, using his hands and mouth like he'd seen guys do on the Internet. Though right now he tried not to think about those kinds of things, because he wanted to concentrate on Javi.

"So good," Javi groaned, placing his hands on Foster's head. He began moving his hips upward, pressing deeper.

Foster did his best to take as much of Javi's cock as he could. He snaked his hand up Javi's belly and then to his chest and nipples, teasing the now hard buds between his fingers. There were so many things he wanted to explore, all at once, now. He wanted to learn all there was to know about Javi. What he liked, what made him make that swallowing, gasping sound other than when Foster ran his tongue along the underside of his cock while he sucked.

Javi's whimpers became more insistent, and Foster backed away, wrapping his fingers around his length. He stroked hard and fast, the way he liked it himself, and Javi came, shaking and writhing while Foster watched the most amazing spectacle of his life.

Javi breathed deeply, his belly raising and lowering, abs quivering. "What do I say?" Javi opened his eyes and drew Foster into a kiss. "A minute and I'll...."

Foster nodded and then groaned when he heard a car slowing outside. He stood and went to his dresser and pulled on some underwear and then a pair of jeans and a T-shirt while Javi adjusted his clothing. "I'm going to take the wet clothes down and put them in the dryer. It's time for lunch, so we'll eat and then I'll take you to your family. I need to talk to them to make sure they're ready to start on Monday."

Javi nodded stiffly.

Foster picked up the wet clothes, giving Javi time to compose himself. "It's okay." He leaned close, kissing him gently. "Everything is going to be okay."

"I wish I had your confidence."

"Foster, we're back." His mother's voice drifted through the house.

He let Javi go down the stairs first and motioned for him to sit down while he continued through to the laundry room, shoved the clothes in the dryer, and turned it on high. When he turned around, he saw his mother standing in the doorway. "We got a little wet so I'm drying Javi's clothes while we eat."

"Why do I think you two got more than a little wet," his mother teased. "Go on and take a rest for a while. We're going to make lunch." She patted his shoulder and left the laundry room, and Foster joined Javi in the living room. He turned on the television and found a rerun of *NCIS*.

"Have you watched this before?" Foster asked.

Javi shook his head. "We don't have a television," he said very softly, like he was ashamed or something. Foster turned to see if he could get any additional information from his expression, but Javi was watching the show and Foster got nothing. Maybe it was just a simple statement of fact.

"I don't watch very much. The best shows are on while I'm usually out milking." He shrugged and sat back, enjoying a few minutes of rest. His eyes drifted closed as he remembered what he and Javi had done upstairs. He was more relaxed and content than usual. Maybe it was the sex, because he couldn't wipe the smile from his face. Or maybe it was having a friend here with him. He realized he hadn't spent time with any friends in a while. Not that he had a large circle of friends to begin with. "Do you have friends?" he asked.

Javi shook his head. "Just my brother and sister. We don't stay in one place long enough to make real friends. The kids play with other kids sometimes, but then everyone moves on...."

Foster thought he might be starting to understand how tough Javi's life was. "I don't have friends either."

Javi leaned forward in the chair. "But you've lived here your entire life." Disbelief was clear in his voice.

"Yeah. But even when I went to school, I got up early, helped with milking, got on the bus, went to school for the day, came home, and had a snack before helping my dad with the evening milking. We did things together, and some nights I'd go to Scouts, but sports was out—it took too much time. I didn't do a lot of activities after school, and it wasn't like the people I knew in school wanted to come to my house to milk cows with me." He shrugged and turned to Javi. "How did you go to school if you moved all the time?"

"When it isn't summer, we have a lady—she's the daughter of a migrant worker, like us, and she went to college to be a teacher, so she travels with the group we work with and teaches us. With her help I was able to take a test to graduate high school a year ago. I work with the kids as best I can because education is their one chance to have a better life."

Grandma Katie came into the room and sat down on the sofa. "I didn't mean to listen in, but I applaud you for that."

"Daniela is so smart. Much smarter than me. She soaks up everything like a sponge. Ricky has so much energy and needs a way to channel it. He likes to build things and figure out how they work."

"It sounds like you care for them very much," his grandmother said. "That's very admirable."

"They're all I have, ma'am. Everyone else, except my mom and dad, of course, comes and goes. The five of us are it." There was no regret or "poor me" tone in his voice. Javi was merely stating a fact that he seemed to have accepted. Not that it was so different from his own life in some ways. Foster didn't move from place to place, but his life had always revolved around the farm.

His grandmother nodded. "This life, one tied to the land, requires dedication, and it can be a harsh master. Whether you own the land or work it, nature is a hard taskmaster."

"Not as hard as my father," Javi said, and Foster shared a brief look of concern with his grandmother. He remembered the marks on Javi's back and wondered just how Javi's father treated his family. He wanted to ask Javi about it, but this wasn't the time, and it was likely Javi wouldn't want to talk about it, judging by the way he'd folded his arms over his chest.

"I've been living on this farm for most of my adult life," Grandma Katie continued. "I married when I was seventeen and have been here ever since. It's a hard life, but a good one."

"Ours is a hard life too, but I don't know how good it is," Javi said, and Foster's grandmother nodded. "I didn't mean to—" He faltered.

"Honesty is to be treasured, young man," Grandma Katie said. "But if you want your life to get better, then you have to make it better." She stared hard at Javi. "No one is going to hand anything to you. My husband bought this land and started the farm. He worked hard for years and years. I raised the children and took care of the house. I also learned how to make something out of nothing, especially the year the garden failed because it got washed away."

"But how do I do that?" Javi asked. "It seems so hard."

Grandma Katie sat back and shrugged. "If I had all the answers, I'd be rich and living the high life in New York. I don't, but I can tell you that we had a plan. We started the farm with a few cows, hoping to raise enough to feed ourselves and get through from one year to the next. Then we built it up, bought more land, and put it to work. We did that again and again. Kids today want it all, and they want everything now." She smiled and leaned closer to Javi, crooking her finger. "The secret that I can tell you is to start somewhere—start small, and build. That's how Walmart started, Meijer, and every other big business you see. They didn't start big—someone built them. And if you put your mind to it, that could be you." Having said her piece, she sat back.

"It's time for lunch," his mother called.

Foster got up and noticed Javi waited for Grandma Katie and took her by the arm. Foster thought it sweet, and he wondered if she'd made an impression.

"What are your plans for the afternoon?" his mother asked once they'd all sat down and passed the sandwiches and salad.

"I'm going to check that the herd has food and water, then I'm going to take Javi back and make sure we can start cutting asparagus on Monday." If the truth were told, he wasn't in a hurry. He liked having Javi there and hoped they were becoming friends as well as… whatever their activities in the bedroom earlier meant. He hoped Javi liked him and that their being together wasn't just sex for Javi. It was special for him, more than just sex. But they hadn't had a chance to talk about it, and at the moment Foster wasn't too sure he wanted to.

They ate their lunch, talking a little as they did. As soon as he was done, Foster excused himself. "I'll meet you out in the yard when you're done." Javi stood. "Just finish eating and don't be in a hurry. I'm going to check the girls, and then I'll be right back. Then we can go."

FOSTER MET Javi in the yard half an hour later, and they got in the truck. "You seem nervous."

"I am, honestly. Sometimes when I come back, I don't know what I'm going to find. Sometimes my father will be gone, other times he'll be sitting around drinking. If he's doing that, the kids will stay out of the way." He turned to look out the side window.

"About earlier," Foster said, getting up his courage. "That was really special." He took one hand off the wheel, and Javi looked at it, smiled, and then slipped his hand into Foster's.

"It was for me too." Javi squeezed, but as Foster slowed, he pulled his hand away. Foster made the turn and pulled into the drive, then parked near a standalone awning. The van was gone, and Maria sat under the awning with Daniela and Ricky. Once he parked and they got out, the two kids surged over to them at a run, surrounding Javi, jumping and grinning.

"Do you remember Mr. Foster? I've been working with him, and on Monday we're all going to start picking." The kids were clearly less excited about that, and Javi went over to where his mother sat, working dough near a stove. They spoke softly in Spanish. Foster didn't understand what they were saying, so he used that time to wander out into the field to look around.

He saw a number of stalks poking out of the ground—some ready to pick and others right behind them. By Monday they'd be ready for a first picking, and the second cutting a week later should work as well, as long as the weather cooperated.

"Is everything okay for Monday?" Javi asked.

"Looks perfect," Foster said, looking around, and then turning back to Javi, where his gaze stopped.

"My mother asked about the clothes," Javi said.

"I'll bring yours back a little later." Foster remembered that he'd forgotten to pay Javi for his work and pulled out his wallet.

"Just add it to what my family makes," Javi said. He leaned closer. "Make sure you give the money to my mother. Dad won't have the guts to ask for it that way."

"Okay." There was so much he wanted to ask, but now was not the time. "There's a park just outside of town, and I was wondering if you'd like to go tomorrow. There are hiking trails and a creek that runs through it with bridges and things like that. Although it's Saturday, I still have to milk and all, but we could go after that." Foster hadn't taken any time away from the farm since his father passed, and he deserved some time to himself.

"Are you sure there isn't someone else you'd rather spend time with?" Javi asked.

"I think we'd have fun. But if you need to stay here, I'll understand."

Javi thought for a minute. "No. I'll walk up to the farm and meet you at eight?" Javi asked.

"Good." Foster grinned and bent to examine the shoots.

"Something wrong?" Javi asked when Foster seemed intent.

"No. But if someone is watching, they'll think we're talking crops." He grinned and stood, excited that Javi had agreed to meet him.

"I'll have to make sure it's okay with my parents if I go with you," Javi said, biting his lower lip and turning back to where his mother worked, his expression shifting to worry. "My mother doesn't know where my father is." He turned back to Foster. "He left this morning with the van, and she says he didn't have work. She's worried he's drinking and then will drive back. Meanwhile, the awning is the only shelter they have. If it rains or gets windy…."

Jesus. What kind of man leaves his family alone with nothing but a flimsy bit of canvas? The kids seemed okay, but they stayed close in the shade for the most part. What really struck Foster was that there was almost nothing, just a couple of flimsy chairs and small tables. The kids didn't have anything to occupy their time. They seemed completely at odds with everything around them, like they'd been stranded in the middle of the ocean. They were surrounded by fields instead of water, but still just as alone.

"They can come back to the farm," Foster offered.

Javi hesitated, and Foster was about to repeat his offer when he saw the red van on the road. It slowed and made the turn into the field, then came to a stop near the awning. Ricky and Daniela greeted their father cautiously, and Foster followed Javi as he approached as well. Foster assumed they weren't sure if he was drunk and were being cautious, but he wasn't sure. The dynamic in the family seemed… off… somehow.

"Mr. Ramos," Foster said as they approached. They shook hands. "I brought Javi back and wanted to check on the crop. Will you be ready to go on Monday?"

"Yes. We'll be ready," he answered. Foster didn't smell anything on his breath, which he took as a good sign. "What are these?" Mr. Ramos snapped, pointing to what Javi was wearing.

Foster answered before Javi got a chance. "He was working with me and got wet. I lent him some clothes while his dry." Mr. Ramos's expression softened, but his gaze still held an intense skepticism, and he kept watching Javi. "If you'll excuse me, I'll let you all have your lunch." He wasn't sure what was going on, but he knew he needed to get away.

Foster said good-bye to Javi as well as Mrs. Ramos before heading to his truck. He opened the door, leaning on it as he watched Mr. Ramos talking to his wife. He could hear the tone, which was firm, but didn't seem angry, thank goodness, though the words in Spanish escaped him.

He got in the truck, turned it around, and drove out to the road. Maybe this whole thing with Javi was a bad idea. It seemed relations within his family were strained at best right now, and Foster was concerned that Javi having any sort of relationship with him would add to that strain. He could hear his father's voice in the back of his head telling him that he was the boss and they were hired hands, and that he should keep his distance and not get involved. But the thought of staying away from Javi made his chest ache and his pulse race, and not in a good way.

CHAPTER 5

THE FOLLOWING morning, Foster got up early and finished his morning chores, grateful that the dairy came to take delivery of the milk first thing. His mother could oversee it, but Foster was glad that it was done. The herd was out in the pasture and they were content. The weather was nice enough right now, and things seemed to be going well. To his relief, the price of milk had gone up a little, so they were making a little more at the moment. That was a financial help, but it could change, or an unexpected expense could wipe out the gain at any time.

"Why do you keep looking out the window?" his grandmother asked after he turned for the tenth time to see if Javi was there.

"No reason," he answered and went back to his breakfast, but he saw the way his mother and grandmother shared a look. He was really beginning to think Javi wasn't coming. "It doesn't matter."

"Doesn't look that way to me. You said you had plans today. They wouldn't be with Javi, would they?" His grandmother leered at him and then broke into a smile.

"Grandma, I think you've had too much coffee. I was going to go into the park in town, and I asked Javi if he wanted to go, but...." He paused, then said, "I don't know if everything is all right with his family. I know it's none of my business and they'll be gone in a few weeks, but it seems strange to me, that's all." He'd seen how quiet and on edge they all were, but what really concerned him were the scars he'd felt on Javi's back. There was violence in Javi's life, and Foster hated that with everything he had.

"You were only there for a few minutes," his mother said. "It could have been a bad day, or you could be wrong. They have a right to their privacy." His mother smiled and motioned out the window. Javi was turning to walk up the drive, carrying a bundle in his arms. Foster finished his breakfast and then got up, meeting Javi at the door.

"Come on in. Are you hungry?" Foster asked.

"No, I'm good." Javi handed him the clothes, and Foster showed Javi where his dry stuff was. Then they went on through to the kitchen, where Grandma Katie proceeded to ply Javi with food.

"What do you have planned?" she asked.

"Foster is taking me to the park. We're going hiking and things." Javi once again ate like he was starving, even though he said he'd eaten. "It's been a while since I had some time just to have fun."

Foster got a small cooler, then packed some sodas and snacks. By the time he was ready, Javi had finished eating. "I'll be back in time for afternoon chores," he told his mother.

"I do know how to bring in the herd and milk, you know," she teased.

"I know. But I worry about you and Grandma." They did a lot, and he hoped they weren't being overworked. Not that either of them was likely to tell him.

"We're fine. It's you we're worried about. So go have some fun." She squeezed his cheeks between her hands, and Foster rolled his eyes.

"I have my phone if you need me," he said, then got out of Dodge.

In the truck, he put on some oldies, and they sang along.

"You like this?" Javi asked when "Mamma Mia" came on.

"Yeah," Foster admitted. ABBA was his guilty pleasure, and he probably wouldn't have told anyone else. But he wanted Javi to know. "Is it lame?"

Javi laughed and turned up the volume.

They reached the parking lot two songs later, both grinning like idiots. Foster pulled in. It was quiet, with just a few other cars there. Tall, thick trees shaded everything. Foster closed the truck door. "My dad used to bring me here." He scanned the area, smiling at the old swing set and monkey bars that he used to play on. They were now painted bright colors. He remembered his dad teaching him how to pump his legs to swing himself, right over there.

"Where are we going?" Javi asked, pulling Foster out of his daydream.

"The path starts there," he answered, pointing, and they walked that way, passing another couple as they emerged from the trail.

"Foster?" the woman questioned.

"Sally?" He smiled as he recognized his high school friend. He hadn't seen her in years. "I heard you moved to St. Louis."

"I did. Are you still at the farm?" she asked, and he nodded. The man next to her hummed softly, and Sally colored. "This is my fiancé, Brad." She giggled happily. "We're just visiting, and I wanted to show him the sights." There was a little mischief in her eyes, and Foster wondered what she and Brad had been up to on their walk. "We came back to tell Mom and Dad." She wriggled her fingers.

"I'm happy for you. Congratulations," Foster said. "This is a friend, Javi. We were just going to take a walk."

"Your dad gave you the time off?" she asked, and Foster shook his head, the smile slipping from his face. Sally placed her hand over her mouth. "Oh, I'm sorry. My mom told me he passed, but it didn't click right away." She pulled away from Brad and gathered Foster into her arms. "Your dad was so cool. Remember how he had the entire class out so Mrs. Philips could show us where milk came from? He took us all around your farm and explained everything. Then he gave us some cheese your grandmother had made."

Foster tried to remember. "That was, like, fifth grade."

"Yeah. But it was still cool, especially when we got to milk one of the cows."

Now he remembered. Sally had been one of the few kids to actually volunteer to give it a try. "I remember. I think the cow had some sort of complex after that."

"I bet she did, after Billy Madison tried to milk her like he was holding a baseball or something. She kicked at him, I think." They chuckled at the memory.

"Dear, we need to get back. Your mother is expecting us," Brad said gently. "It was nice to meet you." He shook hands with both Foster and Javi. Foster and Sally shared a brief hug, and then the couple walked toward their car.

"She seems nice."

"He needs to pull the stick out of his butt," Foster said and then laughed. "God, that was awful. I only met the guy for five minutes, but he seemed...." He shrugged, and they continued toward the trailhead.

"Did all that really happen, with the cow?" Javi asked.

"It did." He'd completely forgotten, and now he wondered what else he'd put out of his mind.

They entered the trail, the leaves thickening overhead, sunlight reaching the ground only in dappled patches.

"Is that the creek?" Javi asked as the gurgle of water caught on the breeze.

"Yeah. It's just up the way." Foster led them to the bridge over the small creek. "When I was a kid, this was where I always left the main path. There's an old one that goes along the creek." He pointed.

Javi walked over to where it began, then took a few steps. "Come on." He grinned and began walking.

"I haven't been this way in years," Foster said as he followed. "There used to be frogs in the low spots, and we'd catch them in Boy Scouts and have jumping contests." He shook his head as he remembered his dad cheering his frog on. The trail followed the creek, and soon the croak of a big old bullfrog reached his ears. He smiled, and a splash followed when they got too close.

They were alone—no voices of other people, no moos of cows. This place was utterly silent other than the breeze and the rustle of the leaves. "I used to think I was the only one," Foster said, just talking off the top of his head.

"You mean like us?" Javi asked.

"Yeah. I used to think there couldn't be anyone else like me and that there was something wrong with me. I remember going to church and praying to be like everyone else." Foster stopped, looking up at the canopy overhead. "Things would be easier if I was."

"Yeah," Javi said, moving to stand next to him, touching Foster's hand. "I never thought about that. I used to wish I could be like the kids of the people we worked for and have a house, sleep in a real bed instead of one that folded out into a table during the day, crammed with two other kids."

"I resented living on a farm for a long time. I wanted a house in town and a dad with a regular job that didn't require me to work all the time too." He'd never thought how lucky he was. He'd never worried about where his next meal was coming from, and he had a nice house with his own room and a mom who did his laundry and cooked for him. "I thought I had it really bad."

"I shouldn't complain. There are migrants who have it worse than us. Some families lose their transportation and can't afford to get something new. Then they're stuck in one area, and they can go months without work." Javi stopped and took his hand. "I had this friend, Maricruz, when I was Ricky's age. Our families traveled a lot together, especially in Southern California and Georgia, of all places. After a year we parted ways because my father got angry at her father. They stayed in California, and we went on." Javi shivered even in the heat, and Foster pulled him into his arms. "I heard later that my dad was drunk and got into a fight with her dad, so they left. He's always got to be the one in charge and making the decisions, even when he doesn't know shit."

"What happened?" Foster whispered.

"When we got to California the next winter, I asked around, but nobody knew anything until I found one of her friends, Juanita Suarez. Big girl who took no crap from nobody. I liked her. She said their truck broke down and wasn't repairable, so they ended up staying. Her dad tried to find work, and so did her mom...."

Chills ran down Foster's spine. "Jesus."

"One of the hangers-on. We get plenty of people who visit the camps, supplying everything that people who want to forget about their lives could use. He apparently took an interest in Mari. She was

71

pretty and sort of quiet, with huge doe eyes that you noticed right off. Next thing everyone knew, she went with him and didn't come back." Javi pulled away, and Foster looked at him blankly. He wasn't sure what Javi was trying to say.

"Was she dead?" he asked.

"She might as well have been. I never saw her again, but everyone in the camp knew that she was most likely hooked and working as a prostitute. That's what happened to girls who went with guys like that. They were full of sweet words, but only pain on the other end."

"I guess I'm missing your point."

"Daniela is pretty and guys have approached her out there, but they have to get past my mother, and by the time that might happen, we're packing up to move on." Javi smirked. "It's one of the only benefits of migrating all the time. Sometimes you get to leave your problems behind." Javi started walking again, fast, and Foster stretched his legs to keep up. "The real shit deal about this is that there's no one to stand up for us. Most people don't see us. All they want is for us to pick whatever they want or hang their drywall, take what they're willing to give, and then go away. Don't stay, don't clog our schools, and don't expect fair treatment, especially from the police." He continued striding down the path that went close to the creek. Foster hoped he didn't slip, but Javi was on a tear.

"What can we do?" Foster asked.

"Do?" Javi stopped and whipped around. "There's nothing you can do. It's all over the country, everywhere. My family and I live in a van, and we generally get paid cash because no one will pay Social Security for people who work for them a few weeks and move on."

"Yeah. You're private contractors," Foster said, almost to himself. Because that was how everyone got around the requirement.

"Exactly. And most migrant workers are illegals, so those of us who aren't get lumped in with them and we get no help. Because we move, school is often a problem. But Daniela and Ricky have to go to school. One year they went to eight schools and learned nothing because they were always behind... until we got the teacher who was willing to move with us, at least part of the year." His voice kept getting louder. "I want a better life for Ricky and Daniela. And for me too. We deserve it, but I don't know how to bring it about. This is all my parents know, and they aren't going to stop traveling. Neither of them has any particular skills. My dad got no more schooling than Ricky has now, and he doesn't see the need for more to pick peaches and cut asparagus. So we'll be here for a few more weeks and then go south a little ways, probably pick beans somewhere until other fruit starts coming in. Then lettuces, maybe pears and apples. Who knows? Head south once again and start all over during the winter. We'll all be a year older, no further ahead, and just as vulnerable." Javi glared at him. "Do? There's nothing you, me, or anyone else can do. It's just the way it is!" His voice echoed off the trees, mixing with the wind, which carried it away.

Javi turned toward the running water, staring as it flowed by. "Things are the way they are," he finally mumbled. "There's nothing I can do to change it."

"Maybe, maybe not. You can change things for yourself if you wanted to."

"You mean leave my family?" Javi asked, turning to look over his shoulder. "I can't do that. As much as I hate the life we lead, never staying in the same place, they need me. What would Ricky and Daniela do if I wasn't there? Should I just leave my mother?" Foster noticed that Javi seemed to have no concern about leaving his father. "For what? What opportunity do I have? I'm a Latino kid that no one is going to trust. I have no education and no training for anything."

"You work hard and you're honest. That goes a long way."

"How do you know I'm honest?" Javi asked. "What if I'm just some thieving spic?"

"What?" Foster stood next to Javi.

"You don't know me that well. I've only worked with you for a few days, and we—" Javi stumbled vocally, his eyes losing their intense energy and hatred.

"So you're telling me...," Foster prompted. "What? That you want a different life, but aren't willing to do what's required to get it?" He caught Javi's gaze in his and held it, not backing down. "I know you're willing to work hard, so come up with an idea like Grandma said and make it happen."

"But my family...."

"Are Ricky and Daniela your children?" Foster shook his head. "They're your father and mother's. They had them and they're responsible for them. If you leave, get an education, make something of yourself, find your own way, whatever... aren't you helping them?"

"You don't understand. The only way we'll survive is if we stick together," Javi said.

"Who told you that?" Foster challenged. "Let me guess. Your father." He knew he was right by the slight sting around Javi's eyes. "He doesn't want you to leave. This past week, who's been bringing in the money? Who's taking care of the kids? You are. While he's out drinking." He hated attacking Javi's father like this and knew very well that it could backfire and Javi could hate him for saying something bad about his dad. "You're the hardworking one, the honest one. Whoever told you that you weren't good enough was so full of shit—" Foster's hands clenched into fists. "You're just as capable as anyone else and can do whatever you want to do."

"Well...."

"Let me ask you this. How long do you think it will be before your dad decides it's time for you to get married? Then what?" Foster knew that answer from the way Javi paled.

"He's already asked." Javi sighed. "I can't leave them because they need me."

Foster had no further arguments and remained quiet. Instead he placed his arm around Javi's waist and gently tugged him closer. "I wish I had answers for you."

"There aren't any. Like I said before, things are the way they are, and it's what I have to learn to accept and deal with. Dreams and wishes are as useful as rain after a hurricane." Javi leaned against him and grew quiet, his posture becoming less rigid, the storm inside lessening, Foster hoped.

"Feel better?" Foster asked after a while as the sun got higher in the sky and the warmth of the day began setting in.

"Yes," Javi whispered. "I can't believe I went off like that."

"Sometimes we all need to let out what's been building up inside." Foster knew one thing: he was going to try to remember how lucky he was the next time he felt put upon and like the weight of the world was on his shoulders. He had choices and opportunities. He had a farm, a business he'd inherited from his father that he could choose to put his effort into and to try to make better and grow. Heck, if they wanted, his family could sell the farm and he could take his life in a whole different direction. That idea wasn't a good one as far as he was concerned, but it was a possibility.

"It's all right." He needed to get his mind back in the here and now.

"Did you mean what you said… about me?"

"Yes. I don't lie." Foster turned to Javi with a smile and guided their lips together. The kiss was gentle, Foster trying to soothe and reassure. Although it was only a few seconds, the heat that simmered below the surface when they were together fanned to life. Javi moved closer, and Foster held him tighter, deepening the kiss as heat built. Foster wasn't sure if it was the sun or from Javi, and he didn't care.

Javi clung to him, tightening his hands around his back, sliding lower to cup Foster's ass.

Foster loved that and shoved their groins together, rocking slightly to add friction.

"Foster."

"Yeah, sweetheart," Foster breathed. His mind was already clouding with desire, and all he could think about was Javi—his scent, rich and woody, his taste, salty sweetness, and the feel of his hard muscle under his hands.

"We're out here on the path, and there are insects buzzing around us." Javi chuckled, and Foster blinked a few times before stepping back. The gnats had started to swarm, so they hurried back the way they'd come. The damn things followed them until they reached the edge of the woods.

The two of them fell onto the grass, laughing. "I'm sorry. I should have thought about that." He'd completely lost track of what was happening around them. If someone had come down the trail, he wouldn't have noticed until it was too late. "I should get the cooler so we can have something to drink." It was indeed getting warmer, and the breeze from earlier seemed to have died away to nothing. Foster got up and jogged to the truck, brought back the cooler, and handed Javi a Coke.

"I guess we got carried away." Javi popped open the can, drank, and sighed. "I never get these." He smacked his lips and looked as though he was holding something special.

"Coke?"

"Yeah. When you don't have much to eat, soda isn't high on the list of things to buy."

It had never occurred to Foster to think of something so… normal as being special. "I guess you're right." He opened his own can and took a sip, wondering what other things he took for granted that weren't part of Javi's world. All he could conclude was that he had a lot to learn and even more to be thankful for.

"I'm sorry things didn't work out on our hike," Foster said. He'd envisioned them being together, walking through the woods, talking and laughing. He hadn't expected to get surrounded by every insect in the state.

"You're sorry?" Javi said in disbelief. "I ruined it. You were being nice, and I went off on a tirade of self-pity." He turned away. "Not very cool of me."

Foster looked around, thankful the park was pretty empty. Then he scooted closer to Javi. "You know, it's okay. You can be angry with your family. I get upset with mine too. God." He looked around. "I used to dream all the time about getting away from here. I wanted to live in a city with a fancy job and a cool apartment, high up, like you see in the movies. Don't know what I was going to do to earn it, but that was how I saw myself." Foster took another drink from his can.

"Why didn't you?"

Foster shrugged. "All I know is that you need to work and figure out how to get away if you don't want to do what you're doing anymore. But I never figured out how to leave home. I went to college for a few years, but it wasn't for me. I passed and all, but I didn't do super well. I thought about driving a truck or something like that, because truckers can earn good money, but I didn't do that either. What I did was stay where I was and work the family farm because it's what I know." He closed his eyes and rested his head on Javi's shoulder. "So I'm one to talk about getting out and making things better and shit. I've done none of it, and I spouted that crap to you. No wonder you got mad."

Javi began to laugh. Foster wasn't sure why, but the sound was big and warm. He lifted his head, caught the mirth in Javi's eyes, and smiled, turning his hands over as a sign of confusion.

"We're a pair, aren't we?" Javi asked.

Foster chuckled. "I guess we are." He got to his feet and tugged Javi to his, then picked up the soda cans and the cooler bag. "Let's wander over there." He pointed to the other end of the park, past the playground equipment.

"Okay," Javi agreed.

They began walking, not quite touching, their hands brushing together occasionally. It was nice, having a friend.

"Do you want to chance it?" Javi asked, indicating a path. The trees weren't as thick, and more sun illuminated the way.

"Sure," Foster said with a smile. He drank the last of his soda and threw away the can. Javi did the same, and then they took the plunge.

The insects seemed to be leaving them alone. This trail led along the near side of the creek. It was better maintained than the previous trail, but still secluded, and they were very much alone.

Javi took Foster's hand, squeezed his fingers, and then released them. "It's so quiet," he muttered.

"I bet it's quieter at night out where you are," Foster said. "There aren't many cars that take that way."

"It is, but with Mom and Dad, Daniela and Ricky, there's enough noise. Dad snores, and Ricky tosses and turns. He has bad dreams sometimes and wakes up screaming. But otherwise it's quiet. I think here I was referring to how I feel, right now, with you. It's quiet in my head. I don't know how else to describe it."

"You're relaxed and content," Foster offered, trying to understand what Javi was trying to explain.

"That's part of it." He turned and stood right in front of Foster, pulling him into a kiss. "I'm happy here with you. I can be myself, and I don't worry about being judged." Javi closed his eyes, kissing him again. "I don't want to think about it or second-guess it. But I'm happy."

Voices nearby forced them apart. "There aren't many places to go for fun around here." Foster tried to think of a place where they could be alone for a little while, but he wasn't going to take Javi to someplace tawdry. He didn't want him to think that he just wanted sex.

"It's all right," Javi said and led them farther down the trail for a while. It made a large loop, so they ended up at the other side of the park and headed back to the truck. They got in, and Foster pulled out and began driving back toward the farm.

"I didn't expect to be returning this quickly." He probably should have planned this outing more carefully.

"Do you have chores at home?" Javi asked.

"Not that I have to do immediately. There's always work, but I have the day off, so to speak." Then it hit him, and Foster made a turn a few miles from the farm, taking a road that headed north.

"Where are we going?"

"There," Foster said, pointing toward a hill dead ahead. "I used to go there as a kid when I wanted to see everything." He turned onto a dirt road that wound around and then went steeply up the tree-covered hill.

"Are you sure this is okay?" Javi asked as Foster slowed to keep them from getting bounced all to hell.

"Yeah. I used to come up here all the time. A guy bought this place a long time ago. He was going to build a house up here, but the first winter made him realize he'd never get up or down in the snow, so he gave up. All that got built was the driveway." Foster reached the top and parked at the edge of a small clearing. They got out, and he took Javi to the edge of the clearing. "This is where he wanted to build the house, I guess."

The view was spectacular. Foster had always understood why someone would want to live up here. "The farm is over there, and if you follow the road in front—" He continued pointing until he saw the speck of red in the field. "That's your van. Muskegon is that way, and Grand Rapids is over there. I always wondered if you could see them from here if the weather was just right, but I never have."

"It's like a map."

"Yeah, it is." The wind blew steadily around them, whistling in their ears. "When I learned to drive and got mad at Mom and Dad, I'd come up here to think. Of course I never came up with anything. But it gave me a chance to cool down and have a few minutes for myself." He tugged Javi closer, then turned to him, kissing him hard.

"Is that why you brought me up here?" Javi asked. "Should I be worried about my virtue?" Foster didn't know what to say and was about to back off, but then Javi laughed and kissed him back. "I was teasing."

Foster colored and turned his head. "I guess I brought you here so we could have a few minutes alone." Now he didn't want to make a move, or Javi would think he'd brought him here for sex or something. Javi placed his fingers under Foster's chin, turning him so they faced each other once again, and kissed him.

The heat from the sun was no match for the pure fire that radiated from both of them. Foster gathered Javi to him, holding him close; hell, he'd have climbed him if he could. Javi tasted awesome, rich and warm, and felt even better. Before Foster realized it, they were moving, doing some weird tiny-stepped dance until the truck pressed to his back. Javi broke away, leaving Foster gasping for air and getting out of the way as Javi lowered the tailgate. Taking his shot, Foster pressed Javi to it, lifting him until his butt rested on the edge. Then he worked open Javi's thin jeans, parting them. Javi stretched, and Foster used that to his advantage, getting the clothes out of the way enough that he could get access to the grand prize within.

Fuck, it was beautiful: long, thick, tanned, head weeping a little. He parted his lips and sank down on it. The flavors he'd tasted during their kiss burst on his tongue as salt, sweet, a touch of sweat… amazing. He took as much of Javi as he could.

Javi quivered and shook. "Holy God," he groaned.

Foster smiled and sucked harder. He ended up gagging a few times until he got the hang of it and figured out how much he could take. By then he was really into the way Javi's cock slid over his tongue and the sounds he made that got carried away on the wind.

"I never thought… it… could… feel so good."

Foster hummed. He had a terrific imagination, but this had been beyond his scope. Fuck, sucking Javi was hot. He pressed him back, working a hand up under his shirt so he could pet Javi's rippled belly and then up farther to work his perked nipples between his fingers.

Javi quivered and held his breath, blowing it out between his teeth. "God, not going to last."

Foster sucked harder, taking as much of Javi as he could, pulling him over the edge and swallowing as Javi came apart, yelling at the top of his lungs out to the entire valley below.

"Damn," Foster murmured after Javi slipped from between his lips. "That was hot." He smiled and climbed up on the tailgate, kissing Javi, sharing his release with him. "I taste like you."

"Like both of us," Javi corrected, thrusting his tongue between Foster's lips.

Foster was so excited he thought his head was going to blow clean off. When Javi grabbed his jeans and slid off the tailgate, Foster watched every move. Soon Javi had Foster's jeans open, and Foster leaned back, shaking with anticipation as Javi pushed up his shirt.

"You're huge, man," Javi moaned, licking along his length. "Damn."

"Is that bad?" Foster asked.

"Fuck no," Javi answered with unabashed delight, grinning before surrounding him with searing wet heat.

"Yes," Foster moaned softly, clamping his eyes closed as he was surrounded and sucked deeper. Few things in life had prepared him for the sheer joy and ecstasy of being taken this way. He held his hips still even though every instinct in his head said to thrust and move.

"Hell, I love this," Javi said, backing away and taking a deep breath before sucking him hard and deep once again.

Foster had little comparison, so he had no idea if Javi was practiced or not, but every touch of his lips or hands set Foster on fire. He wanted this so bad.

He'd been looking up at the sky, but shifting his gaze to Javi, watching his cock disappear between his luscious lips, was nearly enough to send him over the edge. He wasn't ready, wanted this to last, but he knew it wasn't going to. Everything was too new and too special for that to happen. "Javi," he whispered between clenched teeth, trying to hold back the pressure that built with each movement and every use of that teasing tongue.

Within seconds he was coming, mind-numbingly hard, gripping the edge of the truck bed to keep from falling backward, quivering like a leaf.

Javi stood, smiling like the sun, and pulled him up. Foster's pants pooled around his ankles as Javi kissed him. The sun shone on his ass, warming it while Javi did his best to heat the rest of him… and he more than succeeded.

"I wish we could stay up here forever," Foster said softly. "Think about it: no chores, cows, families, fathers…. Leave everything down there alone. Just the two of us here, above all the cares that wait for us."

"You're a poet," Javi teased.

"No. I'm just a guy who spends a lot of his time wishing for things that will never come true."

"See? They don't do us any good," Javi said, reiterating what he'd said by the creek.

"That's where you're wrong," Foster argued, stepping away to pull up his pants. "Without dreams I'd have nothing. See, I dreamed that someday a handsome guy would come into my life and sweep me off my feet, showing me what was possible. Someone like me, so I wouldn't be alone all the time. And here you are." Foster fastened the catch of his pants. "I know I sound kind of dumb and innocent, but that's what I feel."

"But I'm going to have to leave, and then you will be alone," Javi said. "I'll be alone too." The longing in his words reached to Foster's heart, touching it before retreating again.

"But I had my dream, and I'll be able to remember it. Besides, if it came true once, then some of the others will as well." He leaned back against the bed, tugging Javi between his legs. "If mine can come true, yours can too."

"I told you, I can't have any dreams. They don't come true for me."

Foster caressed Javi's cheek. "Doesn't this seem like a dream to you? Did you ever think you'd be here with me… up here… alone?" Cold slowly crept into him. What if this wasn't as important to Javi as it was to him? They were young guys with raging hormones. What if this was just that for Javi and no more? Foster released Javi and stepped back. "It's all right."

"I don't know what to tell you. None of my dreams ever come true. I stopped letting myself think of anything but tomorrow and what we're going to need to survive. If I dream of lovers and happy homes, they aren't going to come true and I'll only end up disappointed." Javi came closer. "But if I did allow myself one dream, it would be you and me, here, right now. There wouldn't be tomorrow or even this afternoon. It would be just now."

"I think that's sad," Foster said.

"That's probably true, but it's what I need to do to survive from day to day. Anything else is a waste of my time and energy. Dreams are definitely for those who can afford them." Javi's expression was granite hard, but it softened as he turned to follow Foster's gaze.

Foster turned him around, pulled Javi in front of him and peered over his shoulder. "That's bullshit and you know it." He felt Javi tense but held him tight. "Close your eyes and think of the one place you want to be more than anywhere else in the world. Not tomorrow, but right at this very second." Foster grew quiet and felt the tension drain out of Javi. "Where is that? If you could be anywhere at all, where would you be?"

"I don't know. Someplace where it's sunny, warm, and there's no work to be done. My mother is happy, singing like she does sometimes when no one is around, and Daniela and Ricky are laughing, playing with other kids in a park like we saw today instead of in the dirt."

"What about for you? Where are you?" Foster realized Javi had included the others, but not himself. "Your mother, brother, and sister are just fine and happy. Where are you?" Foster clarified, and Javi leaned back into his embrace. The wind slowed to a breeze, swirling around them, and Javi placed his hands over Foster's.

"I'm right here. This is where I want to be."

Foster nodded and said nothing. He didn't want to press Javi for more. Instead, he closed his eyes, rested his chin on Javi's shoulder, and stayed still, not wanted to break the spell he'd woven. There was nothing to interrupt them. They were above everything for a little while, and if being here gave Javi the peace he seemed to need, then he'd stay up here as long as they could.

FOSTER DIDN'T move until both he and Javi were sweating from the heat between them. Then and only then did he slowly move back so the air could circulate. "We should go back."

Javi nodded, saying nothing as he stepped away. Foster put up the tailgate and then opened his door to get in the truck. Javi did the same, and Foster started the engine, holding Javi's hand while the engine got the air-conditioning going. He didn't want to say anything that would pop the bubble of contentment that he felt, so he simply squeezed Javi's hand and then leaned over, kissing him softly. Then he straightened, put the truck in gear, and slowly began their descent back to reality.

They went back to the farm, checked that everything was okay, and then had some lunch before getting back in the truck to take Javi back to his family. He wasn't sure why he was anxious about it. Maybe it was because he was happy that Javi seemed to be happy.

As he drove, the contentment that had surrounded them dissipated like fog in the sun, and by the time he made the turn toward the Ramos family van, Javi was as keyed up as Foster had ever seen him.

Foster pulled to a stop and got out. Javi was already ahead of him as Carlos Ramos rounded the front of the van under a head of steam, his expression thunderous.

"Where were you?" he demanded.

"I was at the farmhouse."

Mr. Ramos's face became redder, his eyes darkening. "I rode up there on my way back from town, and they said you had gone to the park with…." He turned to Foster. "You said you were going up there to work, not spend the day running around the countryside." He broke into Spanish at that point, but Foster didn't need to speak the language to know what was being said. The tone told him everything. Then he said in English, "You lied to me and to your mother."

"I was only having some fun," Javi said weakly in the face of his father's anger. Foster wasn't close enough to tell for sure, but he wondered if his anger was fueled by some form of alcohol. "You know, what you have when you take the van into town to drink, leaving the rest of us here."

The hand movement was so fast, Foster barely saw it. The slap rang out over the land. Javi jerked back and to the side at the sting and the power behind it. Foster stared, unable to immediately process what had happened. Javi's father had slapped him, hard, and he was rooted to the spot. Javi turned away from him, and Foster averted his eyes, but not before he saw Mr. Ramos seething in front of his son, spitting rapid-fire Spanish at him.

Foster couldn't move. He could hardly believe what he'd just witnessed. His hands clenched into fists to strike him back and then relaxed once again. The last residual glow of sex still lingered in him, and he wondered if all that anger had been because Mr. Ramos had seen something in them. If Foster stood up for Javi, would that confirm Mr. Ramos's suspicions? That thought, mixed with embarrassment for Javi, made him turn away, wishing something would happen to break the tension and give them all something to change the center of attention. Javi must be humiliated right now, and Foster wanted to do something—anything—to make that go away and to somehow not make it worse. Anger, fear, resentment, and confusion all mixed together, warring inside him for a few seconds as he tried to figure out what to do. This was Javi's family, and he didn't have a right to get involved. Yet Javi was his friend and he had been hit. Foster's heart pounded as the basic fight-or-flight war took place inside him.

He took a step back and then another. He wasn't worried that Mr. Ramos would hit him, but he thought that if he left, maybe the fuel for Javi's father's anger would go along with him. Their day had started out so wonderfully and now it was ruined. He turned and reached the truck in a few steps, reaching for the chrome door handle. But not touching it.

"Respect!" Foster snapped at nearly the top of his voice. Something had clicked inside him. He whirled around. "Respect!" he said again, glaring at Mr. Ramos. Javi had stepped away from his father, whose Spanish diatribe had ceased.

"Stay out of this, boy," Mr. Ramos said.

Foster paused for a split second as the "respect your elders" training his mother and grandmother had taught him reared forward, but then he continued forward. "On this farm, my farm, we respect each other, and that means you respecting your son."

"This is none of your business."

Foster stopped, stood straight and tall, staring into huge, reddened eyes. "This is my business. You are on my land, and I am your boss." He stared and saw Mr. Ramos blink. "You are here on my land because of my good grace. And you will start work on Monday based on that same good grace." He took yet another step forward, entering Mr. Ramos's personal space, and waited until he took a single step back. Foster had seen his father do that when he wanted to get the upper hand with someone, and damned if it didn't do the trick here. "On this farm we do not hit, and I will tell you this: my farm, my land, is dry. No alcohol. That means if you want to work for me, the drinking stops now. I can smell it on your breath."

"What I do...."

"Respect, Mr. Ramos. Respect for me as the landowner, for your wife and family, your son. That is how we live and work on this farm and how you will behave. Am I making myself perfectly clear? As for today, I asked Javi to come along with me. We went to the park, and I asked him to come as a thank-you for the hard work he'd done for me this week. You have a great son who works hard and cares for his family." Foster looked over at Javi's mother and siblings, who stared back at him in what Foster could only describe as disbelief. "You will respect them while you are on my land, working for me."

"Have you paid him for this work? I haven't seen it," Mr. Ramos countered.

Foster shifted and curled up his lips at the smell of the older man's breath. "I paid him directly. He's an adult and can make his own money. He isn't required to give it to you." Foster took yet another step to assert his dominance. "You will remember where you are and who you work for," he added levelly. Then he turned, schooling his expression, and walked over to where Javi's mother stood with the other kids.

"I'm sorry, Mrs. Ramos, for any inconvenience or hardship I've caused you." He took her hand for only a second, and she nodded once. Then Foster walked toward his truck. "Javi is welcome at the farmhouse anytime." He turned to Mr. Ramos. "I think it would be best if he communicated with me for the family from now on." Foster yanked open the door and got inside.

He started the engine and turned the truck around, then jammed the accelerator to the floor, scattering dirt as he peeled out on his way to the main road. Foster held the steering wheel in a vise grip as he drove back to the farm. He was so angry at Javi's father, and at himself for initially turning away. But now he understood that he'd needed to think. His first reaction had been to hit Mr. Ramos for hitting Javi, but that wouldn't have gotten him anywhere. He banged the wheel with his hand. Javi was a good person, and he deserved better than the life he had with a controlling, drunk father. Where all that stuff about respect had come from, Foster wasn't sure. All he'd done was say the words and the rest had tumbled out. It seemed to do the trick. But now he worried that he might have made things worse for Javi.

As he approached the turn into the farm, a new idea crept into his mind. What if Mr. Ramos decided to leave? Foster could find others to pick the asparagus; that wasn't an issue. What really worried him was that he'd go down on Monday morning and find the field empty and the red van gone.

Foster parked in his usual spot and got out. He thought about going inside, but his emotions were too close to the surface at the moment, and he couldn't risk his mother or grandmother wondering why he was so upset. So he went into the equipment shed, grabbed a hoe, and trudged to the garden. There were always weeds to pull, and he could at least take his frustration and worry out on them.

He worked for a good hour or more, losing track of time. By the time he slowed down, the garden was weed-free, and he'd checked over the strawberries that were beginning to fill the plants.

"It should be a really good crop," his grandmother said as she came up behind him. Foster nodded and stepped back.

"You can't fool me, kid. Whenever you come out here on a Saturday afternoon to do battle with weeds like they're an invading army, it means you're either being punished for something—and you're a little old for that—or you're mad as hell." She walked between the rows. "Do you want to talk about it?"

"No," he answered flatly. "I need to think about what we're going to do." Foster hoped he managed to cover his worry as being about the farm rather than about Javi.

"All right," she said. "Have you checked that we have a spot at the market? If you're going to cut this week, we have to see what we're going to sell on Saturday."

"It's all set. You and Mom will go to Grand Rapids on Saturday, and I'll manage things here for the day."

She continued watching him. "We made labels for the jam, so we're going to take some of that as well. Lord, I hadn't realized how much we had. We had so much fruit last year, and we kept on using it."

"Good. That can help. When we see how well it does, we can decide how much of our fruit crops to sell and how much to make into preserves." He was very concerned about putting additional pressure on his mother and grandmother, but his answer made his grandmother smile. She was very proud of her preserves and jams, but they took a lot of time to make.

"What you're going to need to do is figure out how to get some help. You can't keep working like this. Milking the herd is hard work, you know that, and so is working the farm portion of the operation. You and your dad managed to get the fields planted before he passed, but how are you going to milk, harvest, silo, and hay all on your own? You can't. You and your dad did things together and split the work, but you're only one person. No matter how hard you drive yourself."

"I know, Grandma. But we don't have the money right now. Dad was borrowing, and though Mom has some of his life insurance money left, if I have to hire someone full-time, we'd go through that money very fast."

"So what are you hoping will happen?"

"Honestly, that the crops do well, and we get enough rain and not too much, so I can sell some of the surplus and that everyone at the market goes ape-crap for asparagus this year and just has to have it. I hope they think your jams are worth their weight in gold, because that's the only way I'm going to be able to work my way out of this bind. The price of milk is up, but yesterday I found out that our taxes went up on the land, so that got eaten away just like that."

She narrowed her eyes. "How much?"

"Fifty percent," Foster answered. He'd been trying to figure out how he could tell them, but it just came out when he started talking.

"That's bullshit," she said. "You give me that bill. I've done this battle before, and I know how to fight shit like that." She stepped closer. "You let me see it when we go inside, and I'll bring the fight to them."

"How?"

"I know everyone in this town, including the worm who runs the assessor's office. I think he needs a little reminder."

"Of what?" Foster asked.

"Never you mind," she snapped lightly in that way she had. "You give me the bill and the information they sent with it, and leave the rest to me." The fire in her eyes was shocking.

"Grandma," Foster said.

"You think I don't have a past like everyone else?" She scoffed under her breath. "Well, I do, and so do other people. You don't know all there is about me." She winked, and Foster rolled his eyes. He did not want to think about his grandmother being hot and attractive. Well, she was attractive, but he couldn't picture her that way. No kid wanted to think of their parents as sexual, and thinking of his grandmother like that made him shiver and wonder if he could somehow wash out his brain to eliminate any residue of the idea.

"Okay." He held up his hands. "You do what you think you can."

"Don't worry. I may be old, but I've got tricks up my sleeve you can only dream about." She struck a haughty pose, and Foster turned away.

"Grandma, I'm going to have to work for hours to unsee that."

She laughed, and Foster gave up, setting the sprinkler on the garden and then grabbing his tools. He turned on the water as he left, hoping it would rain again soon. The forecast called for some on Sunday and then for Monday to be nice. If it was right, he was getting some luck in the weather department. He hoped it held in other areas as well. They were going to need it.

"Your grandfather used to say that farming was as close to God as any man could come."

"Not a minister?" Foster asked.

"Nope. Farmers. He always said they prayed more than anyone alive—first for rain, then for sun when there was too much rain, sometimes for a freeze. And then for warmth and spring. Mostly he said they prayed to be able to make it through the year so they could survive to the next one. This is our life, and yeah, sometimes we get ahead, but mostly we pray."

"Then how did Grandpa survive?" Foster asked.

"He had me," she answered with a smirk. "How do you think? This isn't a life that you can do alone. It requires a partner, someone to help in the good times and support you during the bad." She watched him closely and seemed to be trying to puzzle through something. Foster's stomach did a flip-flop and a chill ran up his spine. "You've always been so busy, but you haven't dated anyone in a long time. You need to go out, have some fun, meet younger people, maybe find a wife, someone who understands what's required of a farmer."

He must have looked as thrilled as if he were having his teeth drilled, because she started to laugh.

"I know. You've been shy that way. But there is someone out there for you, and all you have to do is meet them and you'll know."

"How?" Foster asked, continuing on to the toolshed, where he put the things he'd used back in their place.

Grandma Katie followed him into the shed. "When you meet them, your heart will race and you'll want to spend all your time with them. They'll make you laugh and cry. They'll tell you stories that will move you, but mostly you'll want to hold them next to your heart and protect them from all the bad in this world." She sighed and smiled slightly. "I remember when I met your grandfather. He was stunning. Tall and strong, swept me off my feet, and I told him to take a hike because I wasn't going to be a farmer's wife. I wanted a different life. But he was persistent, and he kept coming around, helping my dad when he was hurt. Harley once picked our garden and hauled the crops to market for my dad when he was too sick to move. That's when I knew he was real."

"You were mean."

She shrugged. "I was a catch, I'll have you know. And you're a catch too." She stroked his cheek. "So find someone who makes you feel the way your grandfather made me feel. I miss him each and every day. That man was something else." She let her hands fall to her sides and left the shed. Foster closed the door and turned to the house. "Oh, and make sure they're good in the sack. That makes up for a hell of a lot." Foster wanted to die right there, instantly. His grandmother continued on to the house, laughing like a loon. Great. His grandmother wanted him to meet a girl and get married.

CHAPTER 6

SATURDAY NIGHT clouds rolled in, and on Sunday it rained all day, slow and steady, just like the weatherman on television had said. Foster wondered if he should send him flowers. He didn't see Javi at all, even though he had hoped Javi would come up to the farm. Of course, his father could be keeping him close, and there was always the possibility that they'd left altogether. Though Foster doubted that, if they were as hard off as Carlos had said when they first arrived.

He got up early on Monday, milked, and met the dairy truck. He'd already hitched the asparagus belt to the tractor, so he started the engine and began the slow trek with the containers up to the field. Foster breathed a sigh of relief when he saw the red van in its usual place. All five members of the family were up and seemed ready. Foster explained what he wanted them all to do and then got the tractor in position with each person in their place. He placed a cooler full of water bottles on the platform near the empty plastic containers. "Only pick what's ready. Next week we'll do this field again, so anything that's too small we can cut then." He started the equipment, daring a glance at Javi and flashing a quick smile, hoping he'd be able to talk to him at some point.

No one said anything about the last time they'd met, but Foster did notice that Mr. Ramos met his gaze, challenging him, but said nothing. Foster hardened his jaw, not allowing himself to be intimidated, and began the very long and boring day.

A day like this, slowly going along the rows, reaching the other end, and starting back, would drive him crazy. Javi worked on one side and his father on the other. His mother, brother, and sister talked among themselves and with Javi, and occasionally their father, but Javi never so much as looked at Carlos, let alone spoke to him.

The tension between them was almost palpable, and Foster felt square in the middle of it. When they stopped for a break, Javi stayed away from Carlos, glaring at him, jaw set. Carlos, in turn, glared at Javi and then at him. Foster had most certainly made an enemy of sorts, or at least Carlos was angry with him. Foster didn't care either way, other than how it affected Javi.

"Are you doing okay?" Foster asked Javi as he handed him a bottle of water.

"Yes," he answered quickly, then moved away. Foster looked up and saw Carlos glaring at them. Foster stared back until Carlos turned away.

"You are challenging his manhood, his machismo, and he will never forgive you for it. He is the head of the family, and his word is law. It's important to his pride, and it's part of our culture. Men are men and they know best. So hurting his pride makes him seethe." Javi glanced away. "He hasn't spoken to me since you left, and he blames me for the way you treated him."

"Then he needs to learn that I'm not going to allow him to act that way on my land," Foster said, then took a drink from his bottle. "He has no right."

"In his mind, he has every right," Javi added softly.

Foster shook his head and took the nearly filled tub from the tractor. He put a fresh one down and waited until Carlos finished a drink of water. "Let's get started again. The sooner we're done with this field, the quicker we can all get out of the sun." Foster got back on the tractor, waited a few seconds for the others, and then started once again.

The sun was fierce and the humidity high from the rain the day before. Foster moved as quickly as he dared in order to get the field done by midday. Sweat ran down his back and arms. He checked on the others, and they seemed to be all right, their attention on their work. Only Javi seemed to sense him watching and looked up, the others intent on their task. Foster stopped again to change the tub, and then they did the remainder of the field.

By the time they were done and Foster had placed the last of the crop in the back of the truck, he was exhausted, and Javi seemed completely wiped out. Foster hoped for some clouds for the next few days or so in order to give them a break from the sun and heat. When he was ready to leave, he thanked them all for their hard work and caught Carlos's gaze, acknowledging him, then got in his truck to leave.

He stopped and put the truck into park, got back out and walked up to Javi. "Would you be available to help me bring your idea of a produce stand to fruition? I need some help building a stand near the corner. There's already a turnoff area, so we could use that." Foster glanced at Javi's father, and he sighed and nodded. Foster figured that was as close to a truce as the two of them were going to get.

"I can help you," Javi said.

"Great. I arranged to have a small shed delivered. They'll bring it tomorrow afternoon. They know where to put it and will set up the basic building, but I need some help fitting it out." There were so many things that needed to get done and not enough hours in the day. But if he wanted to sell produce at the farm itself, he needed a place to do it.

"All right." Javi was tense, and Foster knew the source. "Once we get something to eat, I'll walk up to the farm and we can go over what your plans are. I can help you figure out what you need to get. That is, if you want my help with that." Javi glanced toward the ground.

"That would be awesome." Foster smiled. "Go ahead and come to the house when you can, or I can come back in an hour and give you a ride."

"Thanks," Javi said, tension still swirling around them. "I know you have things to do, and I appreciate you taking the time." He was being very formal in the way he spoke. "I'll see you then." Javi glanced to the side, and Foster didn't need to follow his gaze to know what was going on. Foster went back to the truck and headed to the farm, calling Mr. Justice's office on the way to tell him to pick up the produce as soon as he was able.

He pulled into the drive and unloaded the truck, weighing each of the tubs to ensure he knew what he had. Foster didn't trust the produce merchant any farther than he could throw the fat man. Mr. Justice's office had said that a truck was in the area and would be there within the hour.

"How did it go?" his mother asked once he was done and the cuttings were safe in a cool room that extended underground.

"Great. They're on their way to pick up, and Javi is coming down. He's going to help me design and build the stand we're going to use to try to sell produce here. I don't know if it will work, but we can only try. If it doesn't, we'll take the produce to the market and use the building for other storage."

She didn't seem convinced. "I'm worried you're trying to do too much. We're going to try out the farmer's market. Shouldn't we wait to see if that works for us?"

"The building is arriving tomorrow, and they're going to set it up for me. Javi and I are going to fit out the interior with some simple display shelves. The shed I got is for display and sales. There are half doors that fold back inside while the bottom half would stay in place. Like I said, if it doesn't work, we can use it elsewhere. We'd just secure the doors."

"All right. I suppose one of us can go out there a few times a day to check on things. It won't hurt anything."

"It isn't like we're going to make a fortune, but there is traffic that goes by the farm, so why not try to make the most of it?" Foster looked around. "Where's Grandma?"

"She went into town."

"Alone?" Foster was a little surprised. It had been a while since Grandma Katie had driven.

"She has a license and is perfectly capable of driving. I let her take my car and made sure she had a phone with her. I offered to go, but she said this was something she had to do on her own. Now go on and eat. I made sandwiches—they're in the refrigerator." She continued on, and Foster went inside.

He was almost too excited to eat, but he had to, and then he would go pick up Javi so they could plan what to do. He had a vision of what he wanted and the dimensions of the shed he'd purchased. So they should be able to design something that would work. He could have done this on his own, but the farm stand was Javi's idea, and Foster wanted to include him in the realization. He also needed help if he was going to get this done.

He pulled out the plate his mother had made for him and sat down with a soda, eating rather quickly. He was glad he did because he'd just finished when the produce truck pulled into the drive. He set his dishes in the sink and went out to meet the driver.

"Afternoon," Foster called. He'd never seen the driver before. "I'm Foster."

"David," the driver said, and they shook hands. "You have some asparagus?"

"Yes." He led the way to the milking barn and down the set of steps off the mudroom to the root cellar. "I put them down here because it's cool." Foster turned on the light and showed David what he had.

"This is nice."

"Picked a few hours ago."

"Let's get it weighed and in the truck." David lifted a tub and Foster got another. It took three trips each, but they got them all loaded and the driver's weights corresponded with Foster's. David gave him a receipt.

"Will I see you tomorrow?" Foster asked. "We're cutting the second field, and if the weather holds, the third on Wednesday or Thursday."

"Sure will. Just call a few hours before you're ready." David inhaled. "I love asparagus."

"I used to. Not so much now." He smiled, and David nodded his agreement. "I feel like I should know you."

"I was a few years ahead of you in school. David Adams. I think I was a junior when you were a freshman. We saw each other in the halls and stuff, but that was about all. You were in the school play that year." David grinned. "No one would ever have gotten me to wear a skirt like that."

"It was a kilt," Foster corrected good-naturedly. "I took so much crap from the guys for that. The girls all talked about my legs for months, so I guess it evened out."

"I bet it did." David handed him a business card. "Call me directly if you need to, and I'll stop by."

"Thanks a lot." They shook hands again.

"This is a cool place," David said as he looked around. "Looks like you've got a lot going on."

"We're trying," Foster said as he walked David to his truck. He said good-bye and watched as the refrigerated vehicle pulled out of the drive and turned onto the main road. Foster went to his truck and took off. He was going to be late picking up Javi.

He met him at the corner and slowed so Javi could climb in.

"I'm glad to be away," Javi said once Foster turned the truck around. "My father's still angry with me, but he's stopped being mad at you."

"Did something else happen between you?" Foster asked.

"Yeah. He fought with Mom because she's tired of him taking the van and disappearing for hours on end. I stepped in, and he turned his anger on me because it's easier. Dad can never stay mad at Mom, but me…. He and I have never agreed on very much."

"For a while my dad and I didn't get along either," Foster said. "When I was a kid we did, but when I got older I resented all the chores and work I had to do. I told him once that I wasn't his slave and that he could do his own work."

"How did that go over?"

"About as well as things did with your dad a few days ago," Foster answered as he turned into the farmyard. "Did you get something to eat?" Foster pulled to a stop and turned off the engine. Javi had nodded his answer, but the rumbling of his stomach told Foster the truth. He turned toward Javi. "How often do you go without so the others can eat?" Javi shrugged, and Foster marveled at him. "Come on." He got out and led the way inside. He opened the refrigerator and got out lunch meat and bread, then made Javi a couple of sandwiches. He'd gotten Javi seated at the table with a plate and a Coke when he heard his mother calling through the open window.

Foster left the house and met her outside the back door.

"I thought you were working," she asked, turning toward the kitchen.

Foster leaned closer. "He skipped lunch so the kids could have more to eat. What could I do?"

She nodded and patted him on the shoulder with a garden-dirty hand. "Of course, dear. Go on and get your planning done. Then we need to augment the herd feed and get ready for milking." The same as every day.

"Sometimes I swear my chest aches when it's milking time," he quipped.

His mother laughed. "That hasn't happened to me in a few years," she teased and shook her head, especially when Foster shivered. He did not need to hear that. "You started it, son. Now go see to your friend." She turned back to the garden, and Foster went inside.

He liked that his mother had referred to Javi as his friend, because that was how he thought of him. He wasn't an employee or a farm worker—well, he was both those things, at least technically. But to Foster he was foremost his friend, and if he allowed himself to think of how they acted the last two times they were alone, maybe something more. Javi had said he liked him. And if the fact that he didn't seem to be able to get Javi out of his head for more than a few minutes at a time.... "All right," he said to himself, pausing with his hand on the back door. He liked Javi; he really did. Something about him touched Foster's heart.

He wanted to let himself think that there was something between them. He wanted that so much, but Javi would be leaving once the crop was in, and Foster figured after the dustup with Javi's dad it wasn't likely they would ever see each other again. The Ramos family returning next year was probably not in the cards.

The weird thing was that the thought alone was enough to take the wind out of his sails. His grandmother had told him how he'd know when he'd met the right person, and what he hadn't been able to tell her—or been willing to admit to anyone—was that Javi made him feel all those things. But as soon as he allowed himself to think it, he knew he was right, and he was in for some heartache in the near future. His choice was to make the most of the time they had or to back away and minimize the damage.

Foster pulled open the door and strode inside. Javi sat at the table, his plate empty, and Foster moved to stand behind him, leaning over his shoulder, wrapping his arms around his chest.

"What if someone comes in?" Javi asked.

"Mom is outside and Grandma went to town." Foster leaned in close, inhaling Javi's rich, earthy scent. He'd made his decision: if he only had Javi for a short time, he'd take it. Foster pulled out the chair next to Javi and sat down. "I wasn't saying we should rush upstairs or something, but I want to spend time with you, and I'm sorry if I made things more difficult between you and your father. I couldn't let him hit you and not say something." Foster took Javi's hand.

"No one has ever stood up for me the way you did, and that's worth weeks of my father not speaking to me. I finally figured out that to my father, Ricky, Daniela, and me are only worth what we can earn for him. We're like his slaves. We work all the time, and he takes the money and drinks a lot of it away." Javi swallowed hard. "You really care about me, don't you?"

"Yeah, I do."

"Why? My own father doesn't. My mom has all she can handle trying to keep the kids fed. And all I'm good for is harvesting someone else's crops and working to try to feed the family. That's all I've ever done. I know that."

"So you think you're not worth loving?" Foster asked.

Javi shrugged, and Foster was about to lean in to kiss him when he heard the back door open. Foster stood, needing some space between them if his mother came in. "Let's go in the office so we can talk some more." Foster grabbed two more Cokes from the refrigerator, not because he really wanted one but because they were a treat for Javi. He led the way to the room off the living room as the back door banged closed again.

Foster closed the office door and opened the window for fresh air. This room faced the milking barn, so they could talk without being overheard by his mother working outside.

"You are worth loving," Foster said, picking up the conversation where they left off. "You work hard because you care about your family. But you can have so much more."

"No. I can't. You've said that before, but I have to help provide for my brother and sister. You saw what my father is like. He's selfish and more worried about his pride than he is about putting food on the table." Javi leaned on the desk. "I know you care, you showed me that, but it would be best if you backed away and let me go."

Foster's breath caught in his throat. "Is that what you really want?"

"What I want doesn't matter."

"Yes, it does. Don't say what you think I want to hear. You need to tell me the truth. Do you want me to stay away and only see you when you're working? I will, if that's what you want."

"I don't want to get hurt," Javi said. "And that's what's going to happen. I know it because I'm already in trouble and I'm going to have to leave."

"You're not alone," Foster admitted. "I would have kicked your father off my land if I'd thought it would have helped you. Hell, I would have fought him if I thought it would make your life easier."

"Like on a school yard?"

"I know it sounds dumb, but I saw red when he hit you. Your father needs to learn that you're the best part of him." Foster leaned over the top of the desk, kissing Javi lightly at first, then entwined his fingers in his hair, cupping his head so he couldn't get away when he deepened the kiss to the point where he could think of nothing and no one else. "I don't think I've ever cared about anyone in the same way

100

I care about you, or felt as helpless around them. I want to make your life better but don't know how."

"You don't have to feel sorry for me. People like me have been taking care of ourselves for many decades now, and we'll continue into the future."

"That's just it, though. I know I can't help all of the people like you. I just want to help you."

Javi chuckled softly. "Sometimes you can't help, even when you want to."

"But...."

"Foster, you have a family of your own that you need to care for, and I have the same. My dad isn't the greatest father in the world, but he's the one we have, and I know that without me, Ricky and Daniela don't have a chance. I want them to be able to lead a better life, so I make sure they go to school. Daniela is real smart, and Ricky can build anything. They have talent, and if I'm around, they'll have a chance to develop that talent. If I'm not, then they'll see nothing better than what they have now."

"So you'll sacrifice what could be a chance for you to be happy for them?" Foster asked.

Javi nodded. "Would you give up what would make you happy for your mother and grandmother?" he countered. "You don't need to say anything because I know the answer, just like you understand what I have to do."

Foster walked around the desk, and Javi wrapped his arms around his waist. Foster cradled his head and wondered what he was going to do. He'd made his choice and so had Javi, so the only decision he had to make was whether he could live with it and be willing to make the most of the time they had together. But he'd already made that choice, and come hell, high water, or heartbreak, he was going to stick with it.

"We should look at what you'd like to do," Javi said softly.

Foster didn't want to release him, but he had to, so after sharing another kiss, he leaned over the desk and explained the layout of the building.

"I think we should keep it simple." Javi paused. "Wait."

"What are you thinking?"

"Do you have something like an old trestle table? The doors split at about table height."

Foster thought and then nodded. "Yeah. There's one in the basement. It's been down there a long time and it's pretty beat up, but I think it's solid. Why?"

"We could use that here, right in the opening. Then we could build two risers to go on top. That way you can put the second row a little higher than the first, so it's visible." Javi turned to him with a grin. "And the risers could be taken to the farmer's market as well. Or we could just make one extra set. It shouldn't cost much, and we could make them so they fold down if you want. Kill two birds with one stone and reuse what you already have."

"That could be awesome," Foster said.

"Can you show me the table? We should measure it to make sure it's big enough and check to see how wide it is."

Foster didn't know. "Now?"

"Sure. If it doesn't fit, then we need to go to plan B."

Foster opened the door and led Javi through the house to the kitchen, where he opened the door to the basement and turned on the lights. "You have to ignore the mess." Foster led the way down, holding the railing on the steep stairs.

"I thought you said this was messy," Javi said as he looked around, eyes bugging. The walls were lined with shelves filled with preserves, pickles, juice, and vegetables of all kinds. "Man."

"Grandma has been putting things up for years. She wants to sell some of her jams at the market." An entire shelf unit from floor to ceiling was lined with preserves—dozens and dozens of jars.

"What do you do with all of it?"

"Usually Mom and Grandma give a lot of the jam as gifts and to the church for Christmas, but this year they didn't have the bazaar so it's all still here. Anyway, the table is right over here against the wall." He motioned toward the back.

"Is that it?" Javi asked, heading over to a long table with jars of screws and bolts as well as other old tools sitting on it. Foster moved the things off it, and Javi looked it over. "It's rough, but if you have a sander, we could clean it up. Is there a tape measure?"

Foster got a yardstick. "The building is ten feet."

"This is nine. Where did this come from?"

"This part of the basement used to be my grandfather's workshop. He built lots of things. Over time most of the tools were taken out to the building we reshingled so Mom and Grandma could have the laundry area. It was also too damp down here. My grandfather made the table as a workbench of sorts."

"Then he'd be happy if we use it."

"I think Grandpa would be thrilled. The hard part is going to be getting it out of here. It should fit, but it's going to be close." Foster knew it was likely that the table had been built down here and had never left the basement.

Javi peered underneath and came up grinning. "The legs come off, so we can definitely get it out." He was still grinning, and Foster wondered what Javi was up to until he came closer, closing the distance between them. Javi pressed him back against the table, the legs shifting on the concrete floor with a bone-grating sound that neither of them paid attention to. Foster held Javi close as he pushed him farther onto the table. From the intensity and heat radiating in every direction, Foster wondered if Javi was going to try to take him right there on the table. Part of his sex-addled mind wondered if that was a good idea, but hell, as long as Javi kept kissing him, he really didn't much care.

Javi tugged Foster's shirt out of his jeans, then slid his hand underneath and over his skin, raising goose bumps that had nothing at all to do with the cool basement temperature.

The bang of the door at the top of the stairs brought them back to their senses. Javi stepped away, and Foster stood, looking down at the state of his clothes and then at Javi before both of them burst into laughter.

"Are you down there?" Foster's mother called from the top of the stairs.

"Yes. We were checking out the old table," Foster called back as he tucked in his shirt. He knew he should be nervous about skulking around like this, but he was too happy and excited to think about that. Once he was presentable, they climbed the stairs, and Foster turned out the lights. "What do you have in mind for the risers?" he asked Javi.

They didn't stop on their way back to the office and closed the door once they were inside. Foster had expected Javi to be more reticent and nervous after the encounter with his mother, but he seemed happy, his face bright with a grin that seemed permanently in place.

"Like I said," he began, grabbing a pencil and sketching his idea on one of the blank sheets of paper. "I don't think it needs to be anything fancy, but we should sand and finish them. That way the wood will be able to stand up to any moisture without getting stained and looking dirty." He stepped back so Foster could take a look.

"I like them."

"They'll only be eight inches high and wide enough to be steady. I was thinking we could make four of them, each two feet long. That way they won't be heavy and you could move them around or remove one from a section if you have bigger things to sell."

"I like that," Foster said with a grin.

"Great." Javi began adding measurements and making some calculations. "This is what you're going to need to make the shelves. I'd use solid wood rather than plywood. It'll stand up to the moisture better and will look nicer."

The office door opened and his mother poked her head in. "Are you about done? It's getting late."

Foster checked the time and groaned. "Thanks, Mom. We're almost done. I'll get the supplies, and hopefully while we're cutting tomorrow, the building will be set up and we can get to work." He was excited about this project.

"Do you need help with the other chores?" Javi asked.

Foster needed all the help he could get. The problem was that the money he had to pay for that help was in short supply. There would be some coming in from the sale of the crops, but in the end, after expenses, he would only get a few thousand dollars. The farm needed more cash flow, and that was why he was doing all of the other projects, but…. "Yes, I need help," he admitted.

"Then come on. Let's get these chores done so you can do your milking," Javi said, and Foster sighed. He couldn't afford to pay Javi for his time, and he was embarrassed to tell him. He'd used up what money he had and what he was expecting had to go toward taxes and to make sure they had enough to make expenses. The milk provided a steady inflow, but….

All these things ran though his head until a headache began to take root. His grandmother was right—he needed to find a partner, someone who could help him, because running the farm on his own like this was wearing him out.

"Okay." He had no choice at the moment. The work had to get done, and he'd have to find a way to pay Javi.

"Then let's go," Javi said and led him outside. "What do we need to do first?"

"Get feed in the barn for the cows for while they're being milked."

"Foster," his mother called from the back door. "There's a storm coming. Warnings are being issued. We should get the herd inside."

"Thanks," he called as she joined them.

"Javi and I will get the feed, and then you can let in the herd," she said. "It's a tight fit, but we can do it."

"Is the barn really big enough?" Javi asked.

"Yes. We usually milk part of the herd at a time because it's easier, but the barn is big enough." Foster led the way upstairs and tossed down a bale of hay. "Put some in each feeder. Two flakes of the bale," he called down through the opening, waiting for Javi before tossing down a few more bales. Javi and Foster's mother got the feed in each stall, then they called the herd and guided each cow into her stall.

Wind whipped through the open doors, and Foster ran to close them as soon as the last cow was inside. His mother clipped each cow into her stall using a cord similar to a heavy-duty leash.

"Where's Grandma?"

"She got home just as I was coming to get you. She's closing up the house."

Foster dug into his pocket and pulled out the keys to his truck. "Can you drive?" Foster asked Javi, who nodded. "Take my truck, go get your family, and bring them here. This storm could be bad, and they'll have more shelter here than out in that field." He handed him the keys. "Tell them to get here right away. They're probably already hunkering down."

"Thanks," Javi said and hurried out. Foster went back to work getting the cows settled. They stamped and mooed loudly, clearly not liking the weather any more than Foster did.

Foster stepped outside, looking up at the sky. Dark clouds raced overhead, with darker, more ominous formations to the southwest. Lightning flashed, followed by more. Foster kept watching as the clouds got lower to the ground. He didn't like the look one bit as more lightning flashed and near-constant thunder rumbled through the air with enough force that he could feel as well as hear it.

His grandmother stepped outside, and he hurried over to her. "I got all the windows closed," she said. "This looks like a whopper."

"Yeah. Did you turn on the television? What are they saying?"

"Severe thunderstorm warning and tornado watch, with lots of wind and chance of hail."

God, that was not what he needed at all. The crops were just starting to grow well and hail would shred them. Enough of it would beat them to the ground. "I sent Javi to get his family. They need better shelter than that van out in the field." He turned toward the sky once again, worrying about Javi's family. He hoped they got here soon.

Foster closed his eyes and proved his grandfather right by saying a little prayer for everything to be okay before hurrying back to the barn. His mother had already started milking. It was more difficult with the barn so full, so it took more time. Foster helped and they got all the milkers going. The cows stomped and moved more than normal, so they had to be careful they weren't kicked or stepped on.

"It's all right, girls," Foster said, keeping up a steady stream of soothing talk even as a crack of thunder nearly had him jumping out of his skin. "I'll be right back," he said and hurried out of the barn. He wondered where Javi was and breathed a sigh of relief when the truck pulled into the drive.

"Where's the van?" Foster asked when Javi's mother and siblings got out.

"Dad went into town an hour ago," Javi said, slamming the door. "The things are in the back."

"Let's get them in the toolshed. The sky is going to open up any second." He raced to the back, pulled down the tailgate, and unloaded the cookstove, then handed it to Ricky. He grabbed the canvas awning that had been thrown in the back, trying not to drag it on the ground. Javi opened the shed door, and Foster put the awning on the wooden floor and hurried back for the poles while the others got the remaining things.

"Take them inside. Grandma is in the house, and she'll get you settled."

"Gracias," Javi's mother said with a worried smile. The wind continued whipping around as the first huge drops of rain hit the ground. Foster got in the truck and quickly parked it in a sheltered location as the sky opened up. He got out and dashed to the barn, getting soaked within seconds. Some drops bounced on the ground. Hail. Foster watched for a second, said another prayer, and then hurried in to help his mother.

"What happened?" she asked when she saw him.

"It's horizontal out there," Foster told her, speaking loudly to be heard over the rain on the roof, shivering from his wet clothes. "Let's get this done."

Lightning flashed and the scent of ozone filled the air as thunder crashed full volume right behind it. "That was close," his mother said as she continued working. "Try to put it out of your mind and continue with the work. The herd is tense enough, and you need to calm them." The words and her tone were in complete disagreement. She spoke as gently as she would to any of the cows.

"Javi's family is in the house with Grandma. I don't know where Mr. Ramos is." Foster went to work. "He said he was going to town and left them with just an awning for shelter."

"Foster," Javi said. "Is there anything I can do to help?" He strode over to where Foster was working.

"Hose down the troughs to make sure we stay as clean as possible. Hopefully this will blow over and we'll be able to put them out again. Otherwise we'll be up to our ears in manure." His mother grinned, and Javi grabbed a shovel. If they had to stay inside, Foster was worried about having enough hay for all the cows. He had counted on keeping the herd out in the warmer weather.

"Thank you," Foster told Javi as he continued the milking process. The rain didn't let up, and it wasn't until they came to the end of the milking process that the drumming on the roof began to lessen. They kept the girls inside, and Foster checked the milk and then peered outside. It was still raining lightly and everything was soaked and dripping. Since he was already wet, he stepped outside and looked around. The house seemed okay, and so did the other buildings. Javi went to check on his family as Foster continued looking to assess any damage. He checked the side of the house where the garden was and stopped in his tracks. One of the huge trees at the edge of the property lay in a heap across the road, completely blocking it. Limbs were scattered all over the yard like parts of the tree had exploded, sending wooden shrapnel everywhere.

Foster was exhausted and there was more work that had to be done. The road needed to be cleared and the limbs picked up and cut to pieces.

"I'll call the county," his mother said. "They can clear the road."

"Will they?" It was their tree, after all.

"Yes." She patted him on the shoulder and went inside. "Now come inside and get into dry clothes."

He sighed and trudged through the rain and mud. His mother met him with a towel in the mudroom, and he stripped off most of his wet things, covered up, and then hurried through the surprisingly quiet house to his room, where he changed and then came back down.

Javi and his family sat in the living room, eyes wide, all looking out through the windows as though watching for their van to appear. "They saw the tree come down. Lightning hit it," Javi told Foster. "It looked like it burst apart."

Foster nodded. "There are limbs everywhere." Including in the garden they had worked so hard to put in. All he could do was hope that not too much damage had been done.

"Come on," Javi told Ricky and Daniela. "Let's go clean this up."

"I'll make some dinner," his grandmother said.

Foster had barely had a chance to feel his backside in a chair and he was up again.

"There are boots in the mudroom. See what will fit everyone," his mother said as they trooped through the kitchen. She stopped Foster with a touch on the shoulder. "I'm going to try to speak to their mother."

"As far as I know, she speaks Spanish."

She patted his shoulder. "She also speaks Mother." She smiled and walked toward the living room, her touch sliding away.

Foster went to the mudroom and helped Javi, Daniela, and Ricky find boots that fit. Most were his old ones, and some were his mother's. Once they had boots, Foster led them outside. The rain had stopped, but water dripped everywhere.

He led them around the side. "Let's pick up the limbs that we can and pile them there." He took them over to a section of the yard near one of the pastures. "Ricky and Daniela, you concentrate on the area of grass. If a limb is too big, call us. Javi and I are going to try to get the limbs off the garden."

Ricky saluted, and Daniela smacked him lightly. "Don't be smart. He helped us." Daniela turned to him. "Ricky would rather draw all of us working."

"And you'd rather be inside reading," Ricky said.

"I have notebooks inside, and some books. If you help, I'll see that both of you get what you want." Foster wasn't above bribery. "And we'll all have a huge dinner."

Daniela nudged her brother, and they walked off, grabbing the first branches they came to. Foster led Javi to the garden and began carefully lifting branches off the tender plants. "It looks like only the part nearest the tree was affected," Javi said. "The rest is leaves." He picked up branches and walked them over to the growing pile.

What worried Foster most was the strawberry patch. Parts were covered with branches. He began pulling them away, layer upon layer, lifting some large branches off the plants. "Some of the plants got crushed," he said, but thankfully most were only covered with leaves and would recover.

After working an hour, they were able to get the branches off to the side. Foster thought they'd come through all right, all things considered. "What about your father?" he asked Javi as they hauled the last of the branches to the pile.

"I don't know. He should know we'll be here when he doesn't find us at the field." Javi looked toward the road. "He should damn well know that everyone was vulnerable during something like that. The only real shelter we have is the van, and he had it." Javi paled as he paused. "What if you hadn't sent me? What would they have done? The wind would have taken the awning, and they would have been stuck in the middle of a field with no shelter at all." The anger in Javi's voice was unmistakable.

Foster wondered if there was a logical explanation. There had to be. "What if something happened to him?" he offered, throwing the last branch on the pile.

"What will you do with all this?" Ricky asked as he and Daniela stared at the huge pile.

"I have a chain saw, and it'll all be cut up."

"What about all that?" Daniela asked, pointing at the heap of green lying over the road.

"Come on inside," his mother called. "Dinner is almost ready."

110

"Thanks," Foster said and waved. He hoped the county would indeed come to clear it away, or after dinner he'd be working until dark to shift the tree. "Let's go. You all deserve a huge meal, and I appreciate all your help."

They walked inside and took off their wet boots, then his grandmother shooed the kids into the bathroom to wash up.

"A tree fell on one of Mr. Dulles's outbuildings," she told Foster. "Crushed it to matchsticks. There are other trees down as well. The emergency management office at the county said they'd get to the tree tonight. They're working their way this way. If we can help, they'd appreciate it."

Foster nodded and took his seat. Mrs. Ramos helped serve, working with his mother like they were old friends. "I think we came through okay." Foster turned to his grandmother. "I took some of Grandpa's advice."

"Of course you did, dear. It's what farmers do in the face of adversity." Once they'd all sat down, his grandmother led everyone around the table in a short prayer.

IT WAS dark by the time Foster heard the beeping of the county trucks backing up near the farm. Javi's dad hadn't made an appearance, and their entire family was becoming worried. Foster's mother and grandmother were figuring out sleeping arrangements. It had already been designated that Javi would be bunking in with him. Grandma Katie and his mother were doubling up so Mrs. Ramos could have Grandma Katie's room for the night, and the guest room was going to be used by Daniela, with Ricky bunking on the sofa. The house was going to be fuller than Foster could remember, and it was nice in a worried and strange sort of way.

Foster had been half asleep when he heard the trucks, but he got out of his chair and pulled on a pair of boots, then headed out to meet the county workers. "How does it look?" Foster asked as he approached.

"This is the worst so far," one of the men grumbled.

"I have a chain saw and can help," Foster offered, stifling a yawn.

"Much appreciated. Do you want the logs?"

"That would be awesome." He could use them during the winter to offset heating costs. "Let me get my saw, and we'll get started." Foster hurried back to the toolshed, turning on the light and making sure the gas tank was full and the chain had oil. He grabbed a pair of gloves and rejoined the men, who were already at work. Foster took a position away from the others and began sawing away branches, chopping the thicker portions into sizes that would fit in the woodstove. One of the men fed the remaining branches into a huge chipper.

The pile of wood grew as the tree was slowly cut down to size. It took two hours, but eventually all that was left of the old oak tree was a stacked pile of wood that Foster would move when it was light and a scattering of leaves and sawdust, along with a stump.

Foster thanked the guys for all their help before dragging himself into the nearly silent house.

"The others are all in bed," his mother said as Foster flopped down into one of the kitchen chairs. She got him a plate, and Foster ate without thinking. His energy tank was extremely empty, and all he wanted was to go to bed.

"Where's Javi?" he asked.

"Upstairs. He offered to go help, but I thought it best that he stay here and make sure the rest of the family was comfortable." She sipped from her mug. "That family is coming apart. His mother doesn't know what to do. She says her husband has been drinking more and more, and they have less and less, no matter how much they make."

"She told you all that?" Foster said.

His mother nodded. "It took some time, but between her basic English and my college Spanish a lifetime ago, we got our ideas across. She doesn't know what to do if he doesn't show up again."

"Does she really think he's gone?"

His mother shook her head. "She's worried and scared."

"We'll need to make some calls in the morning. Someone will have seen or know something. For now we can give them a good night's sleep. It isn't like we'll be able to pick tomorrow with this rain. The fields will be too soft. But we have to pick on Wednesday or we'll lose part of the crop."

"I think they need work and the money that comes with it." He could tell his mother was at as big a loss as he was regarding what to do. They would have to go to bed and figure things out in the morning. Hopefully Mr. Ramos would return from wherever he'd gone, and they would all be able to get some answers.

Foster finished eating in silence, and his mother took care of the dishes. "I'm going up to bed." He groaned as he stood. "I'd better check the herd first."

"I did while you were working. Ricky helped me feed them, and they're fine. So go on to bed. The girls are fine, and they've settled down now that the storm has passed. We'll give the pastures some time to dry in the morning before turning them out into the upper areas." She shooed him out of the kitchen, and Foster walked quietly through the dark living room where Ricky was asleep, curled on the sofa.

He went up the stairs and to his room. Javi sat at his desk reading one of Foster's books.

"You could have gone to bed," Foster said.

"I was waiting for you." Javi closed the book and set it aside.

Foster peered over at the copy of Clive Cussler's *Treasure*. "That's one of my favorites. My dad gave it to me years ago. He and I shared a love of Cussler's adventure stories."

"I like them too. I get them at yard sales when I can," Javi said.

Foster picked up the book and handed it back to Javi with a smile before turning and heading out to the bathroom. He showered and brushed his teeth, grabbed his robe from the back of the door, slipped it on, and headed to his bedroom.

Javi sat on the edge of the bed, staring at him nervously. Foster closed the door and locked it quietly, relaxing back against the closed door. He wasn't quite sure what to do at this point. He'd waited awhile to have Javi in his bedroom once again, behind a locked door.

113

Javi seemed as nervous as he was. "I don't know. Your family...."

Foster stepped closer. "It's all right. We need to sleep." He took off his robe and climbed into the bed, waiting to see how Javi would react.

Javi didn't move, just watched him with dark eyes, searching for something—Foster wasn't sure what. He watched as Javi took off his shirt and slid his pants down over his hips and past his legs, his cock relaxed in its nest of black curls.

"You're so beautiful," Foster whispered. When Javi came closer he reached from under the sheet, his fingertips just glancing over Javi's smooth hip. He raised the sheet, and Javi climbed into bed. Foster lowered the sheet and rolled onto his side, pulling Javi to him.

A few years earlier his parents had replaced the furnace. At the time Foster had lobbied heavily for them to add air-conditioning, and he was so glad they had agreed, especially with Javi's warmth pressed up to him. "Are you going to be all right?"

"I don't know. My father is gone, and we may be stranded." Javi rolled over to face him. "He left hours ago and should know to check for us here."

"In the morning, we'll check to see if he came back, and then we'll ask around town. Someone will have seen him." Foster tried to be soothing, gently caressing Javi's belly. "I've thought a lot about having you here with me." He pulled Javi closer. "I think about it at night when I'm alone." Foster lightly kissed Javi's shoulder, his salty heat bursting on his tongue. His cock stiffened, and Foster parted Javi's legs, drawing their hips together. Javi answered with his own excitement.

"We can't do this now. What if someone hears?"

"The door is locked, and as long as we're quiet...." Foster didn't want to push Javi into anything, so he backed away slightly. He took a deep breath to calm his excitement, prepared to roll over and try to get some sleep.

Javi leaned closer, wrapping his arms around him. He felt so good. Foster swallowed a moan and kissed him hard, his excitement growing by the second. They didn't talk, but that didn't stop Foster from saying what he wanted to with his hands. He kept them in constant contact with Javi, caressing him, letting them roam over his hips, thighs, and back, memorizing each contour, even the scars that marred his lover's otherwise smooth back. Those marks threatened to bring the anger at Javi's father that had simmered just under the surface for days back to the forefront.

He pushed that aside and concentrated on Javi. Those marks were part of him now, and that was enough for Foster. He traced them with a finger, and Javi shivered in his arms.

"I know they're ugly," Javi whispered.

"No. They're part of what makes you who you are." Foster smoothed Javi's hair away from his face. "I hate what he did to you, and I'm not a fan of your father, but they aren't ugly." He tugged Javi down into a kiss, but Javi stopped him.

"I don't know what I'm going to do when I have to leave," Javi whispered.

"I suspect things will go back to the way they were," Foster said, swallowing around the lump in his throat. They likely would for him as well, except he didn't want them to. His life had changed, and his heart had been opened to something he didn't want to let go of.

"Is that how you really feel?" Javi blinked a few times, tilting his head slightly, questioningly. "That things will just go back to the way they were?"

Foster sighed, his excitement draining away, replaced by impending loneliness. "What other choice do I have? You'll be gone, and I'll go back to taking care of the farm."

"You do that now," Javi said.

"No. Now I take care of the farm and look forward to when I can be with you. It doesn't matter if we're hiking at the park or reroofing the shed. It all seems better with you around. Like I can get through the days because you're there." Foster knew that would be gone, and then he'd have nothing but the work, day in, day out, for as long as he could see.

"And you think it will be any different for me?" Javi asked. "I'll go back to the same life I had, living with my family in a van, or God knows where, but I'll be thinking of you and what you showed me." Javi crushed Foster to him. "At least I'll have what I remember of you. That's the only thing that no one can take away from me. But my life will never be the same."

Foster closed his eyes, holding Javi against him, almost feeling as lonely as he would once Javi was gone. It sort of felt like he was already gone. "Do you think this is all because we're the first gay people we've gotten to know?" Foster asked.

Javi lifted his head, eyes burning with fire. "Do you think I don't know my own mind or what I feel?"

"Don't get mad. I was just asking if this could be…. I don't know. I know what I feel, too, and I don't think it's because you just walked into my life. There's something about you. The more I learn about you, the more I like you and care about you. It's like everyone is wearing a mask, and you took yours off for me and really let me see you. And because you did that I could take off my mask too." He hoped he was making sense to Javi, because he was barely making sense to himself.

"Yeah. I hide part of who I am from everyone, even my parents and family. I hide that I like to read and that I'm smart from the people we work for. They don't want a farm worker who sees their mistakes. All the people who hire us want are dumb wetbacks who will pick their crops, keep their heads down, and say nothing about how they're treated or how much they're paid. Some places don't even see us. They hire people to find the workers, pay them, and then the middleman pays us. So we never actually see the person we're working for." Javi squirmed, acting like he was trying to get comfortable. "It's been a long time since I've slept in a real bed."

"We all hide some things," Foster said lamely in an effort to cover the fact that he couldn't get his mind around what Javi had told him.

"I know. But you can be smart and no one thinks you're a threat. If the farmers think I'm smart, then they start to worry about a farm worker uprising or something. So I keep my head down and do what they expect."

Foster wished like hell he could make all that go away for Javi. But he was only one person, and he knew he couldn't change the world. "I don't understand why you don't leave and look for a better life. You could have one—I know you could."

Javi didn't answer, and Foster continued holding him, figuring this conversation should probably come to an end. He wasn't going to convince Javi.

"If I did leave my family, where would I go?" Javi finally asked.

"You'd stay here," Foster said. "I need help on the farm, and we could look into getting you into community college or something. You're smart, and that would be a start for you."

"But here I'd be just another farm worker. I wouldn't be moving any longer, but that's what I'd be."

"You'd have a home and a chance to do what you wanted to do… and you'd be here with me." Foster finally let the words pass his lips regarding what he truly wanted. "You'd stay with me."

"As what?" Javi asked, sitting up. "You mean you'd tell your mom and grandmother about yourself… about the two of us?"

"Yeah," Foster said with false bravery. The thought scared him deep down, but he'd do it.

"And what if they turned on you? This farm was your dad's, so now it really belongs to your mom. What if she doesn't like that you're gay? What if she kicked you out and decided to sell? I'd be without a family and so would you. We'd have nothing and be nowhere." He crossed his arms over his chest. "Is that what you want?"

"I'd only ask you to come here and stay with me if I were honest. I wouldn't let you come here as a secret or something," Foster said.

Javi nodded. "It's a lot to ask or expect. I only know one thing, and it's a lot to think about giving it up. If I left, my father would never forgive me. He'd say I was abandoning my family."

117

"The father who left his family alone in a field with a storm coming up," Foster countered more loudly than he intended. He wished he'd kept quiet when he saw Javi's stung expression. Foster pulled back in his mind and listened to what he'd said, cringing slightly. His own father hadn't been perfect, and they hadn't always gotten along, but he wouldn't allow anyone to criticize him, so why did he think it was okay to criticize Javi's father? "Sorry."

"My dad is still the head of the family, and I can't change that. To leave would mean that I was turning my back on them."

"And you can't do that," Foster said flatly. Javi had made that clear enough. It didn't seem to matter how many times they talked about and around this, it always came back to the same thing: Javi had to leave in order to help support his family, and Foster wished he'd stay here with him so they could figure out if there was a future between them. As it was, they had no future after the next week or so.

"Would you leave your mom?" Javi asked, and Foster had to admit that he wouldn't. He'd put his own hopes and dreams aside because taking care of the farm and his family was important to him. How could he ask Javi to be any less to his family? Maybe he was just now getting it. He had a farm and a place to call home; Javi lived in a van. That didn't mean his family meant any less to him or that the van was any less a home. It was small and cramped, but it housed Javi's whole family. So that was home, and just as hard to leave as the farm would be for him.

"I think I understand now." As much as he hated it, because he wanted what he wanted, Foster had to accept the situation. "I can't expect you to be any less of a man than I am, just because you live in a van and move from place to place. I want more for you, but for your mom and Ricky and Daniela, you are the provider for the family, just like I am here."

Javi seemed to relax. "It doesn't have anything to do with how I feel about you. And before you ask, I'm still trying to figure that out. It's going to feel like someone carved part of me away when I go, but it's what I have to do."

"I think I get that now. I wanted you to stay because it would make me happy."

Javi chuckled. "It would make me happy too, I think. But there's more than just my happiness at stake." Javi kissed him, cutting off further discussion and short-circuiting his brain. Foster had figured tonight was going to be quiet, but Javi quickly showed him that he had very different ideas. "I'm not going to waste the time we have," Javi mumbled, and then the time for talking was over.

CHAPTER 7

"ARE YOU ready to go?" Foster asked his mother and grandmother, grabbing his coffee. The sun had yet to make a full appearance. "I have a tub of asparagus with bundles already weighed out, and three dozen jars of preserves that we labeled. They're in the car along with the risers Javi and I built. Use them for display."

"Yes, dear," his mother said. "We also have a tablecloth, change, chairs, and a cooler with lunch and water. I think we're set for the duration."

"Awesome." He was about to do the milking. "Did I give you the receipt book?"

"Yes," his mother said indulgently. "Don't forget to water the garden. The lettuce is really starting to take off, and if it gets enough water and sun, we may be able to start taking it to market in a week or two." Greens were always some of the first things to be planted, and they were ready for market quickly.

"I know." He was also hoping to get the stand at the farm up and running.

"What do we do if someone else has asparagus for a better price?" Grandma Katie asked.

"Meet their price, but I bet at two pounds for five dollars, we'll be the ones setting the price." He really hoped so. "Just be yourselves and talk to people. Don't sit there and wait for people to stop. Engage them, laugh, be the people you are every day."

"Huh," his mother said. "I thought we just had to sit there and take the money."

Foster wasn't sure if she was being serious or not. What shocked him was that she seemed to be. So he decided to ignore the remark.

"The people who do best at any market are the ones who talk to people and tell them about what they're buying. Let them know that the asparagus plants are original, heirloom variety, not genetically altered modern ones." He turned to Grandma Katie. "Tell them about your preserves and how you make them." Foster stood and opened the cupboard, then pulled out a box of Club crackers. "Open a jar and give them a taste. Keep it on ice. The cool thing is that if they like it, they'll keep coming back."

"I don't know about this," Grandma Katie said.

"Remember how you got the assessment squared away?" Foster asked, and she nodded. "Don't do that." He chuckled, and she swatted at him. "Be their grandmother. Everyone will buy something from their grandmother." He finished his coffee. "I hope you have some fun."

They both seemed skeptical but got up to go. "We'll be fine," his mother said. Foster wondered if she was reassuring him or herself.

"I know you will." He hugged them both, and they put the dishes in the sink. Then they all walked out to the yard. Foster watched as they got in the truck, his mother driving, and then he headed to the barn to start the milking.

"FOSTER," JAVI called as Foster was just finishing up for the morning, turning out the girls. The dairy was scheduled to be there soon. They had enough tank space for two days, which meant they could make it until Monday morning.

"I'm in here." He closed the door and began the process of cleaning out the barn. He started with the shoveling and then began hosing everything down. "How's your dad?" Foster asked.

Javi shrugged. "He's not too good. You know he was at a bar during the storm and got into a fight with another man, right? His eye is still swollen shut, and his arm and shoulder are bruised up. He was able to work yesterday, but he's really sore still."

"He's lucky. It could have been worse." Foster reminded himself that he needed to have a final talk with Mr. Ramos about drinking. It was not allowed if he was going to stay here, on or away from the farm. He'd caused enough trouble.

"He says he's going to stay close and isn't going to go to the bar anymore. There isn't any beer or anything at the van, either. I checked." Obviously Javi was as concerned as he was. "What are we doing today?"

"I thought we'd open the stand. I made some signs that we can use, and I got some flags to get attention." Foster was trying to make the most of his venture, but he was nervous that nothing would come of it.

He got some of the asparagus bundles he'd kept back, leaving the ends in water. He also got a case of preserves, and then they carried all of it out to where he'd set up everything the day before.

After opening the upper doors, he set up the table and attached the box for the money to the back of the table. "It looks nice."

"Yeah, it does. Now we'll see if anyone stops." He kept telling himself that if this didn't work he wasn't out anything. He looked up and down the road, and of course it was completely deserted. Not a car to be seen anywhere. He sighed and walked back toward the house.

"What else?"

"Nothing." He finally got a chance to relax a little. The dairy arrived, and he helped them take delivery of the milk. Then he was free for a few hours, and dang if it didn't feel nice.

"Can we go somewhere?" Javi asked.

"Not really. With everyone gone, I need to stay close by in case something happens." Or more accurately, in case someone stopped by his stand. "Do you want to play video games? I have a Wii with some fun games. Have you played before?" Javi shook his head. "Okay, then let's go have some fun." He led Javi inside and got some snacks and sodas. They sat in the living room, and Foster explained the rules of New Super Mario Bros.

Of course Javi was awful to start with, but he caught on fast. "Good hand-eye coordination," Javi quipped as he quickly got the hang of the game. Foster hadn't played in quite a while. At least since before his father passed.

He sat there on the living room floor, the controller in his hand, staring. "I never thought…. But everything seems divided now. It's how I think of things—before and after my dad died."

"Is that how you'll think of it when I have to go?" Javi asked, turning away just in time to die in the game. "It's how I'll remember things. At some time in the future, I'll play video games again and remember this time, right here, before I had to leave you." Javi placed the controller on the floor next to him. "Are we being stupid to let things get so serious so quickly? We're kids. I'm twenty, and you're a few years older. We both have our whole lives ahead of us, and this is our first love…. At least it is for me."

"I know what I feel, and Grandma would tell me to hold on to what I have. She told me her first love was Grandpa, and that they had amazing years together. He died when I was twelve, and she still misses him." Foster squirmed across the floor to get closer. "I think we're setting ourselves up to get hurt. But I wouldn't change that for anything. I decided days ago that I'd take what we had and be happy with it. If you have to go, then I'll deal with it when you're gone. But not now." He leaned closer. "I saw this movie a year ago. It's about a boy and a girl. She has cancer that took part of her lung, and she meets a boy who lost part of his leg to cancer. They meet and fall in love." Foster wiped his eyes. "I get emotional when I think about it. You see, they all expect her to die. She uses oxygen and has trouble breathing. They both know she could go with an infection, but they fall in love anyway. And they're happy and content. I really like that part of the movie. They deserve happiness." Foster smiled.

"What happens?" Javi asked. "Does she die?"

"Not on screen. Though she does eventually die. His cancer comes back. That's the kicker. They were prepared for her to go, but not him. But she survived it, at least as far as the movie went. And I figure if she can survive the loss of her best friend, and love, then I'll figure out a way to do it too."

Javi blinked. "How can I be your best friend?"

Foster shook his head, chuckling. "That's what you got from what I just said?"

"No. But I can understand how you love me, because I love you. But I don't understand how I can be your best friend. You've lived here all your life. There have to be others you've known for years. People you're close to."

"Not really. I had people I was friends with in school, but they went on to college. I stayed in touch with some of them, but I ended up on a different path. They've all graduated now and gone on to bigger things. I'm still here, milking cows like I have all my life. Besides, I feel like I can tell you anything."

"Yeah?" Javi asked. "Then tell me something no one else knows."

Foster thought. "Okay. I smoked pot once. I was seventeen and I bought a joint at a school dance. I didn't smoke it there, but I came home and smoked it behind the toolshed. Made me silly as shit, and I had to hide from my mom or she'd know I'd done something. So I sat behind the shed, staring up at the stars until I was so cold, I couldn't stand it anymore. Then I came inside, ate a bunch of food, and went up to bed."

Javi looked aghast for two seconds and then burst into a grin. "Is that all?"

"No. Grandma came in once I was almost asleep, sat on the edge of the bed, and asked me if getting high was worth it."

"She knew?"

"Grandma doesn't miss much. Then she said that when she tried it, she got sick. And danged if I didn't wake up in the night, sick as a dog. She never told my mom and dad, and I never touched the stuff again."

"You were such a bad boy," Javi teased. "That sort of stuff is all over some of the camps. People want to forget how miserable they are. Sometimes, especially in Southern California, there are a lot of other drugs too, and that means some really bad dudes come along with them. About two years ago I saw one of these men, Julio Mendez." Javi curled his upper lip. "He was talking to Ricky, and I saw him give him a small plastic bag. Ricky took it and then hurried away. He was only twelve, and Julio decided he was old enough to try whatever crap he was pushing." Javi's eyes blazed. "I raced in, stared Julio down, and shoved back the bag, pressing it to the dealer's chest." Javi looked down at the carpet. "They were jelly beans."

"What the hell?"

"Exactly. I felt like a real idiot and stammered away, taking Ricky with me. I felt so stupid."

"Was he really a dealer or a guy being nice?" Foster asked.

"That's what I wondered until I learned that was Julio's bit. He gave the kids candy in plastic bags so they would be less afraid of him, and then later he slipped stuff into it. Soon he was giving them the drugs, directly in the same plastic bags, and they were some of his most loyal customers." Javi looked up. "Do you see now why I can't go? Who will protect Ricky and Daniela from predators like that if I'm not there?"

Foster had already accepted what would be. He kept hoping that by some miracle Javi would change his mind. But that wasn't going to happen. They both had responsibilities, and Javi couldn't release his any more than Foster could just walk away from the farm. He got to his feet and tugged Javi to his, leaving the television and game where they were, forgotten for the moment and unimportant. "I know you need to protect them." He didn't want to talk about Javi's family any longer, or his own, for that matter.

His mother and grandmother would be gone for hours yet, and they had the house to themselves. Foster couldn't remember the last time that had happened, so he led Javi upstairs and down the hall to his bedroom, closing the door behind them.

Foster sat on the edge of the bed, tugging Javi between his legs, encircling his arms around Javi's waist, resting his head on his chest so he could hear the beat of his heart. Javi ran his fingers through Foster's hair, and he closed his eyes, taking in the gentle sensation. "I want you to know that this is so hard for me."

Foster lifted his gaze to Javi's. "I don't doubt it. Sometimes our hearts want one thing and our heads another."

125

"It isn't that. I'd love nothing more than to stay, stop moving around all the time, so I could build a life and a home. My head wants it, my heart wants it, but that doesn't mean I can have it." He leaned down, brushing his lips over Foster's. "I learned long ago that we can't have what we want. That's why I stopped dreaming. Dreams got me nowhere." Javi pressed Foster back on the bed. "Right here and now is about all the dreaming I can allow myself to have."

Foster nodded, deepening the kiss. Words were useless at this point. He'd laid his cards on the table, weak as they were, and so had Javi. Things were the way they were going to be, and no amount of wishing and dreaming was going to change that. Maybe Javi was right and he needed to accept things as they were and take today for what it was.

Javi climbed on the bed, and Foster fell back on the mattress, bringing Javi along with him. Foster tugged at Javi's shirt, pulling it off, breaking their mind-throbbing kiss only long enough to get Javi's and then his shirt off before returning with ravenous need. As soon as he let go of the dreams and the hope, he was left with the present, and Foster determined he was going to make the most of every second. No more wishing and dreaming. He was taking what he could right here, right now.

Foster shimmied out from under Javi. He shucked his shoes and pants, gazing heatedly at Javi the way a predator stared down its quarry. He wanted him—his body ached for him, cock throbbing incessantly in his pants just from looking at him. This was his Javi, and they had their time together. He was going to take it all in, remember every moment, and impress every sensation on his mind. He never let his gaze shift, and once naked, he went to work on Javi, letting his shoes thud to the floor and then tugging Javi's jeans down his legs, and they joined the growing pile on the old braided rug.

Then he climbed back onto the bed into Javi's waiting arms, kissing and holding him, chest to chest. Instantly his blood raced, especially when Javi pressed him down onto the mattress, pressing their hips together. Foster had noticed that when they were together, Javi always managed to stay on top. Not that Foster minded, but

Javi had done it the night of the storm as well as the first time they'd been in his bedroom. Now when Foster tried to roll them to get on top, Javi stopped him with a concerned look that had Foster wondering why.

But then Javi ground his hips to Foster's, sliding their cocks together, and Foster's thoughts went out the window, just as Javi most likely hoped they would.

"You feel so good," Foster said softly.

"So do you," Javi said, licking and sucking along Foster's neck and then to his left nipple, nipping it slightly between his lips. Foster arched his back, gasping softly. "I want you, Foster."

He stilled. "You mean, like…."

Javi slid his hand between them, gripping his cock. Foster pressed up into the sensation and gasped when Javi's hand went lower, pressing and tapping lightly at his entrance.

"I've never done that," Foster said, stating the obvious since he hadn't ever done any of the things he'd done with Javi before.

"I know. I haven't either, but I want to be with you that way," Javi whispered, and Foster nodded. He wanted to be as close to Javi as he could. "Do you have slick stuff?"

Foster nodded and looked to the bedside table. Javi pulled open the drawer and rooted around until he found Foster's bottle of unscented massage oil. It was all he had, and he hoped it would work. "Do you think it will hurt?" Foster asked.

"If it does, I'll stop," Javi told him. "I never want to hurt you." Javi set the bottle on the table. "I know what it's like to be hurt." Foster found his hands on the scars on Javi's back. He didn't want to think about how he got them, even though Javi had told him. The anger and pain they brought to mind were not helping to keep the happiness and excitement up.

"You know I'd never hurt you either," Foster said, and Javi nodded, cutting off conversation once again. Javi was very good at keeping Foster's mind occupied with pleasanter things.

Foster heard the snick of the bottle. He felt Javi lean over him, and then his lips were back, kissing, tempting, increasing his amazement that he could feel so wonderfully alive. His skin heated wherever Javi touched him. He could be happy forever being touched like this, that little caress up his hip, the way Javi ran his fingers down the center of his chest, making Foster hold his breath, wondering if he was going to go further, sliding along his cock. Maybe he'd grip it or even stroke him a few times. Javi seemed in the mood to tease, and Foster growled, wanting more so very badly.

A gasp—Foster was surprised it came from himself—was followed by a moan when Javi pressed a finger to him. He continued his teasing, and Foster purred softly. At least that's what it felt like in his throat.

"Is this okay?" Javi asked in a whisper. "I want this to be special."

Foster hummed and nodded his assent, a touch worried but still wanting more than what he was getting. He tensed when Javi entered him. It was only a finger, but he still expected it to hurt. "Oh," Foster gasped in surprise. It felt a little funny, but not bad. When Javi moved, he moaned softly, but when he touched a certain place, Foster's eyes crossed. He held his breath as little stars shot behind his eyes. "What was that?" he whimpered.

Javi shrugged but did it again. "Did I find something good?"

"You sure did," Foster whined. "Do it again."

Foster gripped the bedding as Javi moved his finger. The second time the sensation wasn't as pronounced, maybe because he was expecting it, but it felt really good. Javi got more of the oil, slicking him up good, then opened him more. By this point Foster was in happy land. So when Javi withdrew this time, Foster turned over and got on his hands and knees. He wanted to see Javi, but he also thought that it might be easier like this for their first time.

Javi pressed him down onto the bed, his hips against his butt and his chest to Foster's back. Warm breath slid along his neck, caressing him until Javi licked and sucked on his ear, running his hands down Foster's arms and hands until their fingers laced. "You are the beautiful one."

"You are," Foster argued.

"No. You give yourself to me like this. It makes me seem special."
Foster turned his head enough to see Javi. "You are special."

Javi nuzzled Foster's neck. "I know this whole thing is a bad idea, but I'll never forget you, no matter what. I liked you when you listened to me, and I fell in love with you when you stood up for me, and now I'm going to make love to you."

"Javi," Foster groaned under his breath.

"That's what this is. I love you and I'm showing you what you mean to me. I have never done this, and I will do my best to make you happy." Javi moved away, and Foster felt cold for a few seconds. He heard the bottle but kept his eyes closed, letting the spell Javi had cast linger over him.

Javi's warmth and touch returned, fitting right where he'd left, chest on Foster's back, cock sliding along his cleft, slipping lower and then pressing to his opening. Foster held his breath, tensing even though that was probably the last thing he was supposed to do. "Relax. It's me. I'm not going to hurt you." Javi sucked on his ear and then scraped his teeth over Foster's shoulder as he pressed forward.

"That scratches," Foster said with a small yelp, and then he realized that Javi had entered him. He tightened as Javi pressed deeper inside and then stopped. The stretch and a hint of pain sent a wave of doubt through him. But the pain subsided in a few seconds, and the spasms of his butt muscles evened out as well. Maybe this would be okay. Javi slid deeper, slowly filling him.

"Breathe," Javi said with a soft, warm chuckle that shifted to a moan when Foster clenched. "Damn, you're hot and tight around me. Feels so good." Javi sucked on his ear again, and Foster leaned back, arching and pressing against Javi. "Does it feel good to you?"

"Yeah," Foster breathed, his head spinning a little. The sensation was overpowering, though Javi was taking it so slow—almost too slow, but he was gentle and caring.

"What do you want?"

"Try moving," Foster said, and Javi pulled back, then slid in and out, driving Foster a little out of his mind. Now that the initial pain was past, he was into it and pressed back to Javi, then pulled away, taking charge.

Javi withdrew, and Foster blinked in surprise. "I want to see you," Javi said, so Foster rolled over. Javi raised Foster's legs, pressing them to his chest, and sank back into him. In that instant, Foster's mind took a detour, and he blinked up at Javi. "We should have thought about condoms, huh?" he asked.

Javi paused. "I've never been with anyone, and neither have you. So I hope—"

Foster tried to clear his mind, but Javi was driving him out of it faster than he ever thought possible. "It's fine." They were both innocent about things like this. He reached up and stroked Javi's cheeks, bringing him down into a kiss.

Their lovemaking wasn't smooth or polished. Things happened and they laughed about them, had fun, and enjoyed being together. This was special. Foster was with Javi in a way he'd never been with anyone else, sharing a part of himself that had always been private and only his. Now it was theirs, something that belonged only to the two of them and no one else. Foster felt special just being here with Javi, and it sent him to heights he'd never known while he was alone.

Their gazes locked, and Foster wrapped his arms around Javi's neck, holding him near and letting go of the last of his control, giving it over to Javi as he stroked him, taking charge of Foster's pleasure.

Foster was a little embarrassed at how quickly he reached the pinnacle, shaking and gasping against Javi's lips as he came with mind-floating intensity, and he liked to think he brought Javi along with him.

He kissed Javi through the pants and sighs of release, holding him tightly as they both spent some time in that land of magic and make-believe where every guy goes after release. It was a place where everything was perfect and the world didn't exist. That feeling only lasted a little while, so he relished it and did nothing to end it early.

Foster closed his eyes, breathing deeply, and sighed, loving where he was right at this moment. The worries about Javi leaving and everything were at bay, and he was simply happy, really happy. So why were there bells ringing? It took him a few moments to realize it was the doorbell. "Damn," he swore and got out of the bed, then quickly pulled on his pants and shirt. "I'll be right back." He leaned over the bed, kissed Javi, and then darted out of the room, wondering what could be wrong. He fastened his pants as he raced down the stairs and was presentable by the time he pulled open the front door, or at least he hoped so.

"Mrs. Dulles," he said, greeting her with a smile.

"I saw your stand, and the asparagus looks wonderful."

"Thank you," he said breathily, hoping she'd think he'd run for the door rather than had just made love upstairs with Javi. He had to stifle a smile at the thought that didn't want to go away.

"Your price is good, and I really want to put some up, so I was wondering if I could get thirty pounds? Your dad always picked the field and then sold it. By the time I remembered to ask, it was already gone."

"I have some now," Foster said, trying to remember how much he still had. "I don't think I have thirty pounds, but we'll be picking more on Monday. I can set some aside fresh and bring it over to you."

"You're such a sweetheart. That would be perfect." She opened her purse and handed him seventy-five dollars. "Monday afternoon?"

"Just as soon as we're done picking." He smiled, and she seemed equally happy.

"I always thought your father should try to sell more of his crop himself."

"I've sold most of what I've picked so far, but I still have the second cutting to make on all the acreage, so I can set plenty aside." He smiled as she turned toward her car.

"I'll pass the word. Should they let you know by tomorrow?"

"That would be nice, so I know how much to keep back."

She walked down the steps and out to her car, waving before getting inside. Foster closed the front door and then set the money aside before hurrying upstairs to where Javi waited for him, smiling when he skidded to a stop, rumpling the rug.

"You look happy," Javi observed.

"Your stand is a hit. Mrs. Dulles saw it and ordered thirty pounds of asparagus for Monday. She says she always forgets to ask but she saw the stand, so she stopped."

"That's great," Javi said as Foster slipped out of his pants and pulled off his shirt, practically diving back onto the bed, giggling and laughing as he gathered Javi into his arms.

"That was all your idea, and it's only the first day. People may not actually buy there, but they'll stop and ask when they see it. That's a win." He squirmed against Javi.

"You were the one to listen."

Foster stopped, staring at Javi. "Don't sell yourself short. It was your idea, and all I did was bring in the building. You thought of it and helped me make it happen, so this is your win as much as mine."

"Okay," Javi said, smiling. "I'm glad it's working out. Did you actually check the stand itself?"

"No." Shit, Foster wondered if he should have done that. "Do you really think people will steal vegetables?"

"If they do, then they need the food a lot worse than you do," Javi offered. "It wasn't like you put that much out there. Stop worrying and be happy. You deserve it."

A horn sounded outside, and Foster groaned. "I guess the afterglow is over," he grumbled and began getting dressed once again. This time Javi did as well. Foster finished dressing and opened his bedroom door. He stepped out and ran to the window in the stairwell, paling when he saw the truck his mother and grandmother had taken that morning. "They're back," he whispered and heard Javi rush to finish dressing. "I'll go down and see what happened." When he turned, he saw Javi jumping into the last of his clothes.

The back door opened and slammed shut. "Foster." His mother's happiness rang through the house, and he couldn't help wondering how long that happiness would last if Javi didn't hurry up and his mother caught them upstairs in his bedroom.

"Coming," he called back, and thankfully Javi joined him. He hurried down the stairs and met his mother and grandmother in the kitchen. "You're back early. Was something wrong?"

"We sold out. We were the only ones there selling asparagus, and people came by the whole time." She handed him a box with three jars in it. "They loved the preserves, and we have orders." She set the box on the counter and opened her purse. "Three hundred pounds of asparagus total for twenty different people—I have their names and phone numbers for next week—and twenty-four jars of preserves." She handed him the money from the day.

"Mrs. Dulles stopped by because of the stand and ordered thirty pounds of asparagus. She's also going to tell others." This was beyond anything he had ever expected. That meant that the second cutting from one of the fields was already completely spoken for, and at a much higher rate than he was getting from the produce merchant. "Are we going to have enough preserves?" There were still jars in the cellar, but they couldn't keep up the preserve business for very long.

"Yes, though I think that we'll be sold out after next week, which is fine. The next batch of fruit will start to come in next month, and we can make more jam," Grandma Katie said with a proud smile.

Video game music started in the other room. "Is that Javi?"

"Yeah, Mom. He walked over this morning, and we got a few things done." He felt sort of lazy telling them that he and Javi hadn't done much that morning while they were at market. "I expect we may get a few more orders between today and tomorrow." The sales of their produce, at the much higher rate than the dealer, would be a nice addition to the farm coffers, and hopefully that interest would translate to the rest of their produce when they brought it to market. At least on that front, things were looking up.

"Is everything okay in the barn?" his mother asked.

"Yes. We'll get things ready for milking in a few hours."

"Good. I think we could all do with a rest after lunch," Grandma Katie said as she got to her feet and began pulling fixings out of the refrigerator. "We're going to make our own today, so call Javi in to eat."

Foster got Javi, who came in and sat down. Foster tried not to look at him and smile every few seconds. It was hard. He was happy—both he and the farm had had a great day—but clouds loomed on the horizon. Foster knew that as sure as he knew that winter would eventually arrive.

CHAPTER 8

THE DAYS went by quickly, between milking and working in the fields. Foster would've liked to have been able to say that he was so busy he didn't have a chance to think about the fact that Javi was going to leave. It had rained on Sunday, and with the threat of more rain on Wednesday, they had worked extra hard on Monday and Tuesday to cut all three fields. They had all been ready, and with everything harvested, Javi's family was leaving the following morning.

"Thank you all for all your work. It's very much appreciated," Foster told them, then handed Mrs. Ramos an envelope with the money they'd earned. He also passed over some of his grandmother's preserves as well as a few books for Daniela and art supplies for Ricky. He'd made a promise earlier, and he intended to deliver on it.

"Gracias," Mrs. Ramos said, taking the money and then gripping his hands. He knew she was not only thanking him for the money, but for taking care of them during the storm. Foster smiled and explained that they were always welcome.

Foster shook hands with Mr. Ramos, who had stayed home the past few days and seemed to be on a more even keel. Then he turned to Javi, wondering what exactly he could say. He blinked a few times and then ended up shaking Javi's hand, saying a simple good-bye, and turning to walk away.

That single action was the hardest thing he had ever had to do in his life. His eyes watered, and by the time he got to the truck, he could barely see what was in front of him. Foster wanted to wipe his eyes, but he couldn't let any of Javi's family know how upset he was. They'd wonder, and he wouldn't put Javi in any danger of being outed. Javi had made his decision, and while Foster hated it, he understood, and he was helpless to change it.

Foster opened the truck door and climbed in, starting the engine after slamming the door shut with more force than was necessary. He turned the vehicle around, glancing in the rearview mirror. Javi stood on the back side of the van, alone. He raised his hand, and Foster watched as much as he dared as Javi got smaller behind him. Foster stopped at the road, turned for one last look, wishing he could look into Javi's eyes just one more time. Then he turned his gaze forward and made the turn onto the road.

Foster wasn't ready to go back to the farm, so he continued on, taking the roads away from home before turning and taking the old drive to the top of the hill. He didn't stop until he was at the top. He got out and walked to the edge, staring down at his home and the red Ramos van, still parked in the field. He didn't move and couldn't look away. If he did, Javi would be gone. Foster knew it was dumb for him to get so upset about someone he'd only known a few weeks. He'd tried telling himself that last night for hours on end, but it had done no good. He'd fallen in love with Javi and that was the end of it.

He wiped his eyes with the back of his hand and continued watching. He ended up wiping his eyes again and again until he could watch no more. He turned and went back to the truck, his shoulders slumping. He knew there was nothing he could do except go back to the farm and to work. Return to the life he'd had before Javi walked into it and turned everything upside down. But he couldn't bring himself to return to the farm, not just yet. Once he did, he'd lose the last hold he had. Up here he could still see the van and he knew Javi was down there.

He couldn't stay up there forever. Eventually he turned away, got in the truck, and returned to the real world. He used to come up here to dream and wonder, to stay above the world. Now, like Javi, his dream was gone. Only work remained.

THE FOLLOWING morning, Foster got up, dressed, and milked the girls. He did his best not to wonder what Javi was doing at that moment and if his family was already packing up to leave. One of the cows was fussy as hell, nearly kicking him twice. He left her for a while, milked the others, and then returned, hoping she'd calmed down. He was able to get her milked, but only after fighting with her for longer than he wanted.

He had never been so happy to be done with milking in his life. He let the herd out and checked on the ones in the birthing area. Two new calves, a heifer and a bull calf, stood next to their mothers, nursing happily. A third cow, ready to birth at any moment, blinked at him. "I know, girl, I'll be happy when it's over too." She went back to eating, and Foster turned away with a sigh.

"Can you help your grandmother in the cellar?" his mother asked from the door as he walked across the yard.

"Sure."

"She's trying to inventory what she has so she can decide how much she wants to sell next week."

"All right. I need to open the stand in about an hour." His days were filling quickly. Foster went inside and found his grandmother in the basement, standing in front of the pantry.

"I think we could sell these and keep these."

Foster grinned. "There are only three of us now, and we use a jar of preserves every two weeks. That's two a month. So we don't need a two-year supply. Keep twelve and sell the rest. When we make more, we can add to it."

"You think so?"

"Yeah. And next week, we're going to raise the price to seven dollars. You have too much work in them otherwise." At this rate his grandmother could make preserves day and night and still not be able to keep up. That wasn't what he wanted. He gently took her thin shoulders. "We're only going to do this as long as you enjoy it. If you don't want to make preserves any longer, then we'll sell the fruit and that can be the end of it. You're so much more important to me than a few jars of strawberries."

"I know that, sweetheart." She patted his hand and moved the last jars over to the other shelf. "I need to go check the garden."

"It's fine. We'll weed in a few days." He made a note that he was going to have to cut hay soon. They'd had enough sun and rain that the grasses and alfalfa would be high enough to get a good first cutting.

"You need to rest too." Grandma Katie walked up the stairs, and Foster followed, turning out the lights at the top. He continued outside and got in the truck, then headed out the drive and turned toward the asparagus fields. He drove as quickly as he could but slowed as he approached. The field was quiet—no red van or awning. Foster made the turn back to the park site, locked the power shed, and turned off the pump and water. That was it. He stood, walking the site that Javi and his family had called home while they were here. Who would have thought that three weeks could have made such a difference in his life? Or that Javi being truly gone would leave such a hole behind right beside the one left by the loss of his father?

He walked to where the grass had been trampled and found a few remnants that had been dropped. The animals would eat them or carry them away soon enough. He wished he'd had the forethought to have taken a picture of the two of them while Javi had been here. Instead, all he had were his memories. He slowly walked back to the truck and went home. There was nothing else he could do.

CHAPTER 9

"WE NEED to pick the last of these strawberries. We're going to market tomorrow, and they're not going to last," Grandma Katie said.

Foster left his mother to pick the cucumbers and went over to the strawberry patch. The mid-July sky was threatening, but he hadn't heard any thunder yet, which meant they had a little while before they had to stop what they were doing.

"I have these quarts ready to go," his grandmother continued. "Can you put them in the cellar to keep them cool for tonight?"

"Sure." He hoisted the cases of strawberries and carried them down into the cooler basement. They didn't wash or touch them any more than they had to. That kept the berries fresh and firm until they got to market. Foster transferred all the berries to the basement and then went back to the field and began picking, being very gentle and careful to only handle the berries once. They weren't huge berries, but they were bursting with flavor and commanded an excellent price. "I think we'll get one more picking this year." He was careful to leave the unripe berries where they were.

"I didn't think so last week, but you're right," Grandma Katie concurred. "Some of the newer plants are even sending out fresh blossoms, which is rather odd."

"They're just running late. We'll water them a little extra and see if we can coax some fruit from them." He'd seen stranger things, and if they got even a small picking in a few weeks, that would help. Foster didn't put strawberries in the stand, but he'd added the other vegetables they had, and it had done well to let the locals know what they had to sell.

Foster kept his head down and worked, plucking berry after berry. "Do we have orders for this week?"

"I believe we need thirty quarts at a minimum," his mother answered. "Do we have enough?"

"I counted forty in the basement, plus what we have here. We can't take any more orders, but we'll be able to fulfill what we took and can sell the rest." They had two bushels of cucumbers, and the beans were coming in. Foster had picked those the day before. Spinach was also ready, and his mother was bent over the patch, cutting what she could to take that to market as well.

He kept listening for the thunder and heard the first rumbles in the distance nearly an hour later. He hauled all the containers down to the cellar, where they would remain cool and fresh for the following day. "We've done enough for the day," Foster said when he returned and helped his grandmother up. She totally amazed him on a regular basis. Nothing ever stopped her.

"Are you sure?" his mother asked, still working.

"Yes, Mom. It's going to rain, and you've done more than enough." They all had. He grabbed the last basket as they went inside, the first drops falling as the back door closed. Foster got the huge pitcher of tea out of the refrigerator, and they all sat, drinking and watching as the rain soaked everything outside. It wasn't a harsh storm or too heavy, but it was just what the fields needed and what Foster had been praying for these last couple rather dry weeks.

He finished his tea and stood, then left the house, dodging raindrops, and headed to the barn. The herd had gathered under the overhang at the back of the barn, standing together for shelter against the rain. Foster took the time to prep for milking, making sure he had everything ready. He'd taken to doing this in the afternoon when most of the farm was quiet. Each feed area was set up with their supplements and feed. He had water in each trough, and everything shone after being washed.

"What's going on?"

Foster jumped, turning to face his grandmother. "Why aren't you resting? You have a busy day tomorrow, and I'm worried that I'm overworking you."

"I'm old enough to know my limits," she retorted. "I'll say something if I'm doing too much." She walked toward him, her steps a little halting. "The one I'm worried about is you."

"Me?"

"Yes, and don't try that innocent routine on me. I have eyes. You've been working yourself to the bone, keeping that stand of yours running, the weekend market, milking, the garden. You never stop to rest until you collapse at night."

"I'm fine," he protested.

"Sure you are. Were you fine last week when you got the check from Mr. Justice and practically took his head off when he paid you at last year's rate?"

"He tried to cheat us, the old bastard," Foster argued.

"Are you sure that's why? Or did you call and raise hell because you've been sulking and miserable and took it out on him? You had his note with what he promised, and now you're going to have to smooth things over with him. Eventually you're going to need him."

Foster groaned softly, cringing at the thought. She was right, of course, and that irked him even more.

"You've been short-tempered and blatantly unhappy for weeks now. You worry about money, work, and then go to your room and stay away from the rest of us. So don't tell me that nothing is wrong. I've been around the block and know something about hurt."

"I really don't want to talk about it." He looked around, hoping like hell the hayloft would catch fire or something just so he wouldn't have to face her intense gaze.

"It's been hard without your father. Believe me, I understand that."

Foster didn't respond and continued hoping for something to rescue him from this situation.

"Does this have to do with Javi?" she asked, watching him. Foster knew any answer would give away his feelings. He'd never been good at lying, and lying to Grandma Katie was impossible.

141

Foster turned away and began checking the feed. At least it gave him something to do, no matter how lame. "I know he became your friend, and that's good, but he's gone, and it's time you made some new friends. This can be a lonely life, and you need people to have fun with."

"Javi was...." He actually began to talk and then lost his voice. His lips were moving but nothing came out.

"He was a friend," she supplied and continued stepping closer. "Or was he more than that?"

"Grandma!" Foster protested.

"Hey. He was something to you. I saw it in your eyes and the way you never seemed to stop looking at him. So what was he to you?" Her tone was so soft, almost pleading.

Foster's legs shook and he wanted to run and hide. "Javi was...."

"You need to say it, sweetheart. Let it out and be honest with yourself. Don't do it for me or your mother. We don't matter. You have to say it for you."

"Say what? That I loved Javi and he went away?" Foster blurted and gasped.

"See?" She shrugged slightly. "That wasn't so hard. Were you and Javi intimate?"

"Grandma," he said again. "I—" He was so not having this conversation with her. The idea of talking about this with her squicked him out completely.

"Okay, fine. Was Javi your first love?" she asked, and Foster nodded. He didn't have the fight left in him to argue with her any longer. "Then that explains a lot." She reached out to him, stroking his arm. "You've been hurting and you thought you had to go through all this alone. You don't, you know."

"How can you be so... blasé about this?"

"What? You're gay. So what? You think you're the first gay person I've known?" She rolled her eyes. "Just because I live on a farm doesn't mean I don't know how things are. We get CNN, remember? I get to watch television, and I like that RuPaul show.

It's hilarious." She laughed loudly. "You don't need to hide from the people who love you."

"But why aren't you mad? We've been going to church, and I've heard for years how I'm going to hell because I'm gay."

"Please. That old windbag doesn't know his head from a hole in the ground. I only go because I have friends there. You really think I listen to that crap?"

"Lots of people do." Foster wasn't sure how to react. At this moment he'd always pictured some sort of fight with tears and maybe a few threats or her telling him how disappointed she was.

His grandmother pulled him into a hug. "Sweetheart, I'm your grandmother, and I love you no matter what. Being gay is part of who you are, and didn't I always try to teach you to be true to yourself?"

"Yeah. But I guess...." He swallowed hard and closed his eyes, letting her hug wash over him. He didn't need to beg trouble or heartache; he already had enough to last a lifetime.

"You miss Javi."

"I loved him, Grandma, and now he's gone and I'm not going to see him again." Foster felt tears stinging his eyes. He'd held them in for weeks, not wanting anyone to know what he'd been going through. It sucked to feel like a black hole had opened in his life and to have to keep it in and remain silent about it.

"Are you sure you were in love with him?" she asked.

"You told me how I'd know, that day when we were working in the garden. I spent hours thinking about him when he was gone, and then when we were together, it was like everything was right with the world. He made me happy just by being here." Foster released the hug and wiped his eyes, embarrassment taking over a little. He didn't want to cry in front of her or anyone—he was a man now and in charge of the farm. "He told me he loved me, and I know he did. I could see it in his eyes, but maybe what hurts most is that he didn't love me enough to stay."

She shook her head. "Sweetheart, love isn't the answer for everything. I know you see it in the movies and on television—love

143

overcoming every obstacle, one way or another, and I'd like to think that it's true. But I'm afraid it's not. The world has a completely different agenda sometimes. Javi left with his family because he felt he had to, am I right?"

"Yeah. I asked him to stay. He could go to school if he wanted, and we could work the farm together." Foster's shoulders slumped. "I had this vision in my mind of Javi and me taking care of the farm, living here, happy together for the rest of our lives. I know it was stupid, but I wanted it. I think about him all the time, and I miss him, especially at night."

"Of course you do. I still miss your grandfather after all these years. And I know your mother will always miss your father. I believe that when you love someone, they never truly go away. You carry them with you in your heart and memories always. Your grandfather is always with me because I take the good times we had together wherever I go." She inhaled, and her eyes hardened. "But I do have something important to say that you need to understand. You're young and you have your entire life ahead of you. I spend a good share of my time remembering the happy times of my life. You need to go out and live yours, meet other people, and see what the world has to offer."

Foster looked around the barn. "This is my world, unless you and Mom want to sell the farm." The idea left him cold. The land was part of him. He hadn't realized it until he said the words and thought about losing it. "But that isn't what I want. Mom keeps telling me that I need to find someone to share the farm with, the way Grandpa had you, and Dad had her."

"Yes. But what's more important is that you're happy, regardless of whether you're with someone or not, and lately you've been working yourself hard, day and night, to keep from feeling and thinking about Javi. A broken heart isn't going to heal by forgetting or running away. You need to deal with it and then let the magic of time take over, because that's the only cure… and maybe talking to those who love you."

Foster hugged her as tightly as he dared. Grandma Katie was a tough old bird, but he didn't want to hurt her. "Thanks."

"You're welcome." She patted him on the back. "I'm always here to listen if you need me. And you need to talk to your mother. She's worried about you too."

"Do you think she'll be angry?"

"No. I think your mother just wants you to be happy." She took a step back, looking into Foster's eyes. "I have a few more things to say. First, you better be safe and use condoms."

Foster groaned. There were many things he could talk about with his grandmother, but this was so squicky.

"Don't even go there. You need to be safe."

"Grandma, Javi is gone, and I'm not going to go out and try to sleep with every gay guy within a hundred miles."

She smacked him on the shoulder. "I should hope not. But that doesn't mean you should be stupid. Anyway, second, you need to live for yourself and be happy in who you are. Doesn't matter if you have someone in your life. So don't hide. Your mother and I will support and care for you no matter what, so just be yourself. Sometimes that's the hardest thing in the world."

Foster wasn't sure how he felt about others knowing he was gay. "I need to—"

"Just be happy with who you are. That's all I want for you. It doesn't matter who you love or marry. Just be happy."

"What about church and all those people?"

She scoffed. "Find a place that you're comfortable with and where you fit in."

Foster swallowed. "What if I tell people and no one wants to do business with me anymore? What if we lose the farm because the dairy doesn't want to buy our milk? Or…." He shivered as the possibilities of what they all stood to lose because of him left him cold. "People around here are conservative, and they all go to the same church we do. They've heard that 'old windbag' Reverend Cartwright for years, and they believe it, so what if they start to act on that and cut us out?"

"Then we'll deal with it. But you can't let small-minded people define you. Just be yourself."

Foster nodded. "But what about…." He sighed. There was nothing anyone could do about Javi. He was gone, and no matter how much Foster missed him and wished he hadn't left, there was nothing he could do about it. "I guess I have to get over Javi, but I don't want to forget him." He swallowed hard, remembering the tender moments when they were alone, standing at the top of the hill as they shared their dreams. "I was never anyone's dream before."

"Yes, you were," Grandma Katie said, and Foster realized he'd vocalized his thought out loud. "You were a dream come true to your mom and dad. They didn't think they could have children and had been trying for a long time. Your mom was about to give up, and they had started to research adopting, but then she found out she was pregnant, so believe me, you were your mother's dream, and your dad's." She paused. "But I understand what you mean. Javi looked at you like you were the center of the world, and he kept watching you, sharing smiles, and when you were alone, you shared secrets each of you has only told the other."

"Yeah, and even when we were working, he made the chores seem lighter."

"Your grandfather did that for me, and I like to think I did it for him."

"So what should I do?" Foster asked.

"Remember the best parts, the warmth and the joy, use it like a blanket, and go on." She smiled and turned, walking away more slowly than she usually did. He watched her go, head slightly bowed, swaying ever so slightly from side to side, not unsteadily, but almost like she was dancing. Maybe in her mind she was. Foster certainly hoped that her memories were happy. Because no matter what he'd said to his grandmother, he couldn't let go. Not yet.

CHAPTER 10

FOSTER SAT on the tailgate of his truck, legs dangling as he looked out over his home below, now colored with the first dots of red, yellow, and orange of fall. He didn't have much time. This was a very busy time of year. He'd cut the last of the hay and that had been rolled into huge bales, which had been covered and sat near pastures where he'd need them. He was going to start harvesting the corn soon, placing it in the silos for the winter. There was plenty of work to be done and a lot that had been completed. Somehow he'd done it—they'd done it.

Loneliness was still a near-constant presence, especially when he tortured himself like this and came up here to the top of the hill. "I'm so stupid," he muttered under his breath. "I need to stop this," he added out loud even as he turned to look toward the edge of the asparagus fields, like he always did. There was no red van—not that he expected to see one, obviously. Javi was gone and it was time for him to move on. That was why he'd come up here. Javi wasn't going to return until spring, if at all. Foster slid onto his feet and closed the tailgate before getting in the truck and driving down the hill, then back to the farm.

"Hi, Mom," he called with a smile after getting out. "What are you doing?"

She straightened up from the garden. "Just getting the last of what there is before a really hard frost kills it off." She picked up her basket and carried it along with her. "We'll have a few weeks for some things yet, but the rest are done, and I thought I might as well glean what I could." She turned to him. "What's got you smiling?" She stroked his cheek. "It's good to see you like that again."

"I'm sorry I've been so...."

"I know." She slipped the basket down her arm. "Do you still miss him?"

Foster chuckled. "Yeah. I want to tell him how well we did at the market, and that the stand, which was his idea, has been a great success." He turned to the stand, which was locked up tight now and all set for winter, but would open again in the spring. He had plans to expand what they grew so he could keep it going longer in the season.

"Foster," she said, and he turned his gaze away from the stand, blinking a few times to bring himself back from his little mind trip.

"I'm sorry." He shifted from foot to foot nervously.

"No. You're allowed to feel the way you want." She shook her head. "This has been hard for me because, unlike your grandmother, I didn't see any of it coming."

"I know." His mother had taken the news that he was gay quite hard. She hadn't been angry, but it had been difficult for her to understand. "But it's part of who I am, and I'm coming to understand that and accept it, just like I have to accept that Javi is gone and isn't coming back."

His mother turned away and groaned. "I've seen you. Every morning when you come down for breakfast, the first thing you do is look out in the yard, and you have this hopeful light in your eyes, and then when the yard is empty, it's gone. I still don't understand it after all this time."

"I dream about him almost every night, and then I wake up and want to hope he's here. Is that so bad?" Foster challenged.

"No. I only want you to be happy. I can learn to accept anything as long as you're happy."

"Including me wanting to be with another man?" He'd talked things over with his grandmother, but his mother hadn't wanted to talk up till now. There had been no yelling or drama, just silence on the subject for weeks. And truthfully, he hadn't needed to talk with her about the fact that he was gay. But now that she'd brought it up....

"Yes, dear. I always wanted grandchildren, but I think a nice son-in-law would be perfectly fine." She smiled.

"I just want you to be proud of me," Foster said, and his mother stopped, her expression registering surprise.

"I'm proud of you each and every day. You manage this farm better than your father did. We're in a better place financially than we were last year, and we should make it through the winter without worry. There wasn't a year that your father didn't worry if we would run out of feed or if we'd have enough money to cover unexpected expenses. We have that now and the debts are being paid down. That's the most any farmer can hope for." She hugged him gently. "I've always been proud of you. This isn't an easy life for anyone, and you took to it and have mastered it."

"This is my home. If I didn't do something, we were going to lose it." That had been unacceptable no matter which way he'd looked at it.

"Go on inside and sit down for a little while. I'll make us some lunch, and you can rest for an hour before afternoon chores. There's always work to do, but taking a little time to rest makes all the difference."

He walked with her, not having the heart to argue and knowing a little time to sit with his feet up would be nice, even if he had his laptop on his lap so he could plan his harvest.

They went inside, where his grandmother had already started lunch, filling the kitchen with the buttery scent of fried potatoes and the spice of sausages. "I thought something hot would be good on a day like this."

"Let me help you," Foster said.

She shooed him into the other room. "I can make lunch." She flicked her gaze at his mother quickly enough that Foster wasn't sure he'd seen it. "Go sit down. I'll call when it's ready."

He went into the living room, turned on the television, and settled into his favorite chair. The recliner had been his father's, and Foster had appropriated it since neither his mother nor grandmother ever used it. He lifted his laptop from the floor next to the chair and settled it on his lap. He ended up ignoring the television as he planned how he was going to get all the corn harvested before the snow set in. He still had some time, but the weather would most likely dictate how quickly he could get the crop in. He would need five clear days to get everything in and set. He was figuring out the order and routine he wanted to use when the phone rang and was answered.

"Foster," his mother said, bringing him the phone. The farmhouse still had one of the old ones with the superlong cord.

"Hello?"

"Foster."

"Mr. Dulles, how are you?" Foster smiled.

"Good. It's been a good year, and from the looks of things, you've had a good year as well."

"I took your advice—treated the farm as a business and looked for opportunities. And they seem to have worked out for the most part." He smiled.

"I'm glad to hear it." Foster could hear the smile in the older man's voice. "I was calling to coordinate the use of the harvester." There was no need for both farms to have a full harvester that would be used just one time a year.

"I was just planning what I was going to need." He talked harvest schedules and plans until he was called to lunch. By the time he hung up, Foster had added tentative dates to his harvest plan, and he was relieved he had someone to work with. He had agreed to help with Mr. Dulles's harvest, and he was getting help in return. Things were really working out.

After ending his call, Foster went in for lunch and sat in his usual place. His mother and grandmother talked softly while he ate and mostly stared out the window at nothing. A car pulled off the road in front of the farm.

"Foster," his mother said to get his attention.

Foster turned away, pulling his thoughts back to the present. "Sorry, Mom," he said softly.

"I was saying that we have enough produce to go to the farmer's market one last time. Katie is going to send some of her preserves, and that should be it until spring. She and I will put up the rest of what's in the garden for us to use in the winter."

"That sounds good to me," Foster agreed. Grandma Katie and his mother had already put up plenty, but a little more wouldn't hurt, and neither would a little extra money. "I was thinking about adding yet another garden area. There's some fresh ground over near the toolshed. I thought I'd till it up this fall, and we could plant squash there. There's room, and they'll be easy to grow and a great fall crop."

"Good," his mother said.

"But no zucchini. I hate that stuff," his grandmother chimed in.

"I agree with that. Everyone grows it, anyway. I was thinking some butternut and maybe one other kind of squash. If there's room, we can see about pumpkins, maybe pie pumpkins or something. But they take a lot of room that we may not have."

The doorbell rang, and Grandma Katie got up before he could stop her. "Probably someone asking about the produce stand." She left the room and went to the front door. No one ever came to that door, so Foster wondered if it was people trying to find souls to save or selling something.

"Foster," Grandma Katie called.

He got up, passing her as he headed to the door. "What is it?" he asked.

"Definitely someone for you." Her smile was wickedly naughty, and he went to the door, pulling it open the rest of the way.

Foster stood stock-still, blinking more than once, not willing to believe he was seeing Javi standing on his porch.

"Foster," Javi whispered. He was thinner and his voice seemed rough, his eyes a little sunken. Foster opened the outer door and waited for Javi to step inside before pulling him into a hug, burying his face in his neck. The scent of Javi, something he never thought he'd smell again, filled his head with warmth, sweat, and a hint of spice.

"What are you doing here?" Foster asked when he found his voice.

"Am I welcome?" Javi asked. "I didn't know where else to go, and I hoped you…. That you'd still want…." Javi moved away. "I should have known this was a bad idea." He turned toward the door, but Foster grabbed his arm. Without thinking, he enveloped Javi in another hug and kissed him, hard, full-on, and with all the longing that had built up during their months apart.

"What happened?" Foster asked after breaking the kiss to breathe and then resting his forehead on Javi's. He didn't want to let Javi out of his sight or far enough away that he couldn't touch him. He was afraid that if he did, Javi would disappear and this would all be a dream.

"Foster, you need to finish your lunch," his mother called, and Foster groaned. He didn't want to share Javi with anyone, even for a few minutes.

"You must be hungry." Foster went to close the front door and noticed an old canvas bag on the porch. He brought it in and set it next to the door. Then he took Javi's hand and grinned like an idiot. "I can't believe you're here."

"I didn't know if I should come." The pain in Javi's eyes put a damper on Foster's inner dance of joy. They stopped in the living room. "Things have been very difficult lately."

"Come on in and let's get you something to eat. Then we can talk, I promise." Foster was curious as hell what could have happened. Javi obviously hadn't had enough to eat in a while. "I'm just glad you're here." He squeezed Javi's hand and led the way to the kitchen.

"I made you a plate," Foster's mother said to Javi as soon as he stepped into the room. Javi pulled his hand away, and Foster let it go. Javi would have no way of knowing that things had changed with his family. "Sit down, sweetheart, and eat."

Javi looked at her skeptically, but he pulled out the chair and sat down. Foster sat next to him and finished his lunch, watching Javi eat.

Foster's heart raced as a mountain of possibilities opened up in his mind. But there was much he didn't know and he had to do his best to keep from getting his hopes up. He didn't know why Javi had come back or what his intentions were. Foster was thrilled he was here, but his heart was guarded. He'd begun healing from when Javi left the last time, and he didn't want to feel that way again.

"How'd you come to be here?" Grandma Katie asked.

Javi ate fast, shoveling in the food. Foster's mother put a glass of milk on the table for him. "After we left here, we drove south to pick beans and then moved north with that crop. We'd been picking almost a month when the crop ended. We picked blueberries outside Kalamazoo for a while, and then we were going south again." Javi continued eating between sentences, and everyone else remained quiet. "My father continued drinking more and more, leaving us alone for longer periods of time." Javi took a long drink of milk then set down the glass. "We got into Ohio, and Dad said we were going on down to Florida, but we ran out of gas because he'd drunk up all the gas money and there was almost no food." Javi kept his eyes down.

"If you don't want to talk about it now...."

Javi shook his head. "We had nothing. Ricky and Daniela hadn't had anything to eat, and my mom was crying all the time. Someone called the government, and they stepped in to try to help. My father refused, and my mother, who'd had enough, told him that she was leaving and getting help." Javi stopped, staring at the table. "At that point, they didn't need me any longer and I was another mouth to feed, so I said that I was going to go out on my own, and that I'd send them what I could to help. So I got rides and walked a lot of the way back here." Javi went back to eating and seemed to have ended his story.

Foster knew in his heart that quite a bit was being glossed over. From the look his mother and grandmother shared, they thought the same thing, and given the way they looked at him with identical raised eyebrows, they expected Foster to find out. He intended to, but what Javi told him would remain between the two of them. The others' need to know would have to go unfulfilled.

"Would you like some more?" Foster asked, taking his plate to the sink. Javi didn't answer right away, and Foster put the last of the potatoes and another sausage on Javi's plate. Thank goodness his grandmother always cooked enough for a small army.

"Thank you." Javi didn't say it had been a while since he'd eaten, but that was obvious by his appetite and the hollow look in his eyes, as if he'd been approaching the end of his rope. Foster sat back down, watching Javi, a mixture of anger, relief, and happiness warring inside him. Anger at the way Javi had been treated by his father, happiness and relief that Javi had gotten away and was here with him. But he kept wondering what Javi's intentions were and how amazing it was that when he was alone and needed help, Javi had come here to him. That had to say something about how deep Javi's feelings for him were. At least he hoped that was what it meant. He needed to stop vacillating and second-guessing. Javi had been here less than an hour, and Foster was already putting himself on an unnecessary emotional roller coaster.

Javi cleaned his plate and his eyelids began to droop. "I appreciate all this." He stood. "I know you weren't expecting me, and I should probably go. I can't impose on you like this."

"Stop that," Foster's mother said. "Foster will take you upstairs so you can get cleaned up and rest. You came here because you knew you'd be safe, and you will be."

Javi turned to him, and heat rose from deep inside Foster. He knew why Javi was here—at least he hoped that was what he was seeing. His mother had to know it too, but she was gracious enough not to push. For that Foster was grateful.

"Come on. Let's get you upstairs." He led Javi through the house, picking up his bag along the way.

"I didn't have anywhere else to go, and I hoped that I hadn't hurt you so badly that you'd come to hate me." They stopped on the landing.

"I missed you so much, but I didn't hate you. You did what you felt you had to do for your family. I understand that, and in your place, I would probably have done the same thing." Foster set the bag on the floor and pulled Javi to him. The heat in their touch only intensified when Javi kissed him, pressing him against the wall.

Foster pushed against Javi, needing to get closer and letting his mind wrap around the fact that Javi was here with him. He didn't want to move, but kissing on the landing was probably not the best move, especially in a house he shared with his mother and grandmother.

Javi seemed to have the same idea and stepped away, both of them breathing like they'd run a race. Foster reached for Javi's bag without breaking their gaze and started up the last set of stairs. With each step Foster could feel Javi's gaze on him, adding heat and excitement with each movement. By the time he reached the top of the stairs, Foster's knees were weak. He turned and forced his mind on the task at hand, which was getting Javi settled so he could rest, rather than jumping him right there.

"I'm going to put you in the guest room."

Javi nodded, some of the light fading from his eyes.

"Talk to me," Foster said.

"You don't want me with you?"

Foster sighed. "I didn't want to force you or make you think you could stay only if you stayed with me. You're welcome here. Not just in my bed, but because we want you here." He took Javi's hand and led him down the hall, where he opened the door to the guest room. He wanted to take him a few steps farther to his room but thought better of it. He said he wasn't going to force the issue and he meant it. "I'll put some towels in the bathroom for you, and if you need anything, let us know. We're here to help."

"Don't you have chores?" Javi asked as Foster set down his bag. "I can't stay here if I don't earn my keep." He looked about ready to fall over any second.

"You can help me later. There will be plenty to do tomorrow." Foster left the room, checked that there were towels for Javi, and put out a fresh toothbrush and other things that Javi might need. When he returned, Javi was sitting on the edge of the bed, looking lost and staring at him.

"Your mom and grandma know?" Javi asked.

"Yes. I was miserable after you left, and they started asking questions. Grandma has been great, and Mom is coming around. Not that she was mad or anything, but she's accepting who I am."

"My family never will."

155

"Is that part of why you left?" Foster asked as he sat down next to Javi.

"Yes. They didn't need me anymore. My mom is leaving my father. She says she can't take his drinking and that she knows divorce is a sin, but she has to do what's best for my brother and sister. I told her it would be a sin for her to stay with him." Javi smiled slightly. "She agreed with me, but it's hard for her to go against the church. And I cannot ask her to do it again." He raised his gaze from his battered shoes. "I have to have some happiness in my life. I probably would have stayed with them if it weren't for you."

"Me?" Foster asked.

Javi nodded slowly. "You showed me that I could be happy. I didn't know what it felt like, and then once I did, I had to feel that way again. This was the only place that I was ever happy, so I came back here."

"I'm glad you did." Foster took Javi's hand. "Don't worry about anything. Just get cleaned up and sleep for a while. You're worn out." He wasn't sure if Javi wanted to talk or rest. "When was the last time you ate?"

"Like, a good meal? Maybe three days ago. I had some money when I left, but not enough, I guess, and I ran out. I slept in one of the cars that gave me a ride, but I was worried all the time too. What if they tried to steal from me or hurt me? I didn't know, but I fell asleep because I couldn't keep my eyes open. That was about two days ago, I think." Javi yawned and Foster pulled down the covers. Javi stood and walked unsteadily toward the bathroom. Foster stayed close and waited. He wasn't sure if Javi could stay awake long enough to get back to bed.

When the bathroom door opened and Javi came out in only a towel, Foster got a good look at what he'd missed for months. Javi was more beautiful, even as thin as he was, than the picture Foster had held in his imagination. He jumped to his feet, gently guiding Javi to the bed. When Javi dropped the towel and slid between the sheets, it took all Foster's willpower not to climb in next to him. Instead, he pulled up the covers as Javi rolled over. That was when he saw the fresh marks on Javi's back.

Foster swallowed hard, pulled the covers up the rest of the way, and leaned over Javi, kissing him lightly on the cheek. Then he turned and left the room. Before going downstairs, he gathered Javi's clothes and thought about getting his bag to see if he had other clothes that needed to be laundered but decided that was too intrusive.

"Mom," Foster said when he got back to the kitchen.

"What are these?" she asked when Foster handed her the bundle of clothes. She took them and nodded. "Javi's?"

"Yeah. He's so tired he could hardly move." Foster lowered his voice. "He's been beaten. It was a while ago, from the look of it, but I think we need to get him to a doctor if we can."

"Ask if he'll go when he wakes up. I'll wash these." She patted his shoulder and shook her head. "How could I ever have missed how you feel about him? It's written all over your face."

"You weren't looking," Foster offered. "And I'm not trying to hide any longer." He went outside—he had chores waiting.

FOSTER CAME back inside after milking. He half expected Javi to join him, but his mother said they hadn't heard a peep, so Foster went upstairs while dinner was being made and peered into Javi's room. It was dark with the drawn curtains, Javi a long, sloping ridge in the bed, his dark hair ragged and longer than it had been the last time Foster had seen him. It didn't look like Javi had moved at all. Foster entered the room and sat gently on the side of the bed. "Javi," he said softly, touching his exposed shoulder.

Javi jerked, sitting up with a start, staring at Foster with eyes as big as saucers. Then he calmed and blinked. "Oh," he breathed.

"It's all right. Dinner is almost ready, and I didn't want you to sleep through it." Foster lightly stroked the smooth skin of Javi's arm. "I can't believe you're here." He leaned in slowly, giving Javi a chance to pull away if he wanted to. Foster's heart delighted when Javi returned the kiss, and he felt Javi's excitement through the sheet

157

as he rubbed him slowly, watching Javi's eyes roll and listening as his breath hitched. Foster's did the same. He wanted him so badly, but had to stop. "I shouldn't tease when I can't do what I want."

Javi paused, and Foster pulled away. He shouldn't do this. Javi had to be the one who said what he wanted. Foster didn't want Javi to think that staying here or being with him, or anything, for that matter, was contingent on them being together. Foster would help Javi no matter what, and certainly not because of something he got out of it.

"What's wrong?"

"Nothing," Foster answered. His leg shook with excitement, and he turned away, because if he kept looking, his resolve was going to slip away. "We need to get ready for dinner." Foster stood, reading the confusion in Javi's expression. "I don't want to push you." He turned and went back to the door. "Mom washed your clothes for you. We weren't sure if you had anything clean with you." Foster indicated the chair by the door where he saw the small pile of clothes his mother must have set there.

"Thank you." Javi got out of the bed, and Foster groaned at Javi's nakedness.

"If you're doing that on purpose…," Foster began and then hurried out of the room, breathing deeply, thinking unsexy thoughts so he wouldn't be sporting wood when he went to dinner. He was so keyed up that it took until Javi came out of the room, and then Foster's excitement rose again, undoing most of what he'd been trying to deflate.

"Are you sure it's okay if I stay for a little while? I can go and…."

"Yes." Even if he stayed in the guest room, Foster would let Javi stay as long as he wanted to. He hoped Javi would want to stay with him, but…. "Just relax."

"Javi," Foster's grandmother said happily when they entered the kitchen. "Did you have a good rest?"

He yawned. "I don't remember falling asleep. But I must have been tired." Javi turned toward the window. "I slept the whole day?"

"Yes, you did, sweetheart. Now take a seat." She placed the food on the table and set a pitcher of milk next to it. "How long were you on the road?"

"About a week," Javi explained. "I walked a lot and got some rides with people. Mostly they were nice."

Foster passed him the potatoes. "I've never hitchhiked."

"I don't recommend it. Some people do it all the time, but when you're a hungry Latino man...." Javi caught Foster's glance and smiled. "I guess we don't need to go into that."

"Did someone hurt you?" Grandma Katie asked.

"No. But they tried. They stopped, and I grabbed my stuff from the backseat. Unfortunately it was raining, so I ended up walking a few miles before I came to a town outside South Bend. I got a hotel, but that took most of my money, and after that... I just kept walking."

"Where did you sleep?"

"If it was dry, in the woods by the highways, wherever I could find a dry place. I knew where I wanted to go and had to get there... well, here."

"You had no place else to go?" his mother asked. "No other family?"

Foster shot her a stern look.

"No, ma'am. I wanted to see Foster. My family...." Javi's thought trailed off, and Foster handed him the platter of chicken. "I'm sorry I intruded. I'll get my things." Javi pushed his chair back from the table. Foster looked at his grandmother, panicking. Then he shot his mother a withering look that made her flinch.

"You'll sit down and eat. Then after dinner you and Foster can talk." Grandma Katie reached for his hand. "You are welcome here, and we're glad you came to us." She smiled, and Javi sat back down.

"Don't worry," Foster said to try to reassure him, patting his hand.

Javi nodded once and began to eat... and eat.

"I do like a man with an appetite," his mother said after a while, most likely trying to make up for her earlier comment. Her backpedaling did little to ease the tension around the table.

Foster had never been so happy to see a meal come to an end in his life. He and Javi left the table, and Foster put on a jacket to go out to the barn. Javi seemed anxious to come with him, so he got him one he could borrow and led Javi out.

"I don't think they want me here," Javi said as they walked across the yard.

"They have questions, that's all." Foster turned to him. "They don't know you like I do or have the same feelings for you that I do." This was all so much more complicated than when he'd just hoped that Javi would return.

"So what should I do?"

Foster pulled open the door to the barn. "Tell me what really happened."

"I did."

Foster shook his head. "You glossed over it, but I saw the marks on your back."

Javi slumped. "My dad was drinking and he got angry."

"Why?"

"He found my notebook."

Foster tilted his head slightly to the side. "What notebook?"

"After I left, I got this cheap notebook that I kept in the bottom of my bag, and I wrote my thoughts in it, about how I missed you and wished I'd been able to stay. Things about what we did and how much I loved you." Javi covered his face with his hands. "I know it was stupid, but I couldn't hold it in, and when my dad was looking for money, he went through my bag and found the notebook."

Ice zinged up Foster's spine. "Oh God."

"I didn't know anything about it until my father got me alone. He was drunk. He took off his belt and whipped me until I could barely stand. He burned the notebook and told me if I ever acted that way again, he'd—" Javi's voice broke. "—he'd cut me."

Foster shivered and it took him a few seconds before he could move. Then he pulled Javi to him. "Is that when you left?"

"Sort of. He disappeared after that, and my mom got the help, like I told you, but I had to get away from him and from them. It was safer, and this way they won't hate me. I had nowhere to go, and all I could think of was trying to get back to you. But I should have known that was too much to hope for."

"You did the right thing coming here. Don't doubt that. Mom and Grandma need a chance to talk to you and get to know you."

"But your mom...."

"She's tough with a heart of gold." Foster took his hand. "They know how much I care about you, and they aren't going to kick you out."

"I'm willing to work and help," Javi said.

"I know, and we're going to need that. It's harvest time, the busiest part of the year. I can pay you a small amount, and I can include a place to live and food. If I phrase it that way, they'll back off, and that will provide time for them to get to know you." At least Foster hoped they'd agree. They had to.

"But what about when there isn't any work?"

Foster scoffed. "There's always work. I'm going to enlarge the garden again, and with more help I can make it even bigger. I also want to see about enlarging the herd. If I milk more cows, I can increase my cash flow, but I can't do any of that without someone to help me."

"So you want me to stay because you need help?" Javi asked.

"No. I want you to stay because I love you. I was torn apart while you were gone, and I'm so happy you're back and that you trusted enough in me to come here." Foster moved forward, his legs thinking for themselves. "I felt so alone without you here."

"All I did was think about you... too much. That's why I had to write things down, because if I didn't I was going to burst with resentment and pain." Javi met him halfway, their bodies fitting together perfectly. "I needed to get back, but I couldn't leave my family." Javi tightened his grip, clinging to Foster, who felt like he was holding Javi on his feet. "But my family left me." There were tears and pain in Javi's voice. "I knew you'd care for me."

"Yes. I'll care for you as much as you'll care for me," Foster whispered.

"But what about your mom and grandmother?"

"I know they'll come to care for you. Give them time." Foster knew he, his mother, and grandmother had plenty of talking to do. But Foster was happy, and ultimately that was what would make his mother and grandmother happy. He stroked Javi's cheek, gazing deep into his amazing dark-chocolate eyes, neither of them moving for a long time.

"Foster, why did we come out here?" Javi asked without breaking their gaze. Just holding each other was a heavenly experience. The tension, worry, and strain of the past few months seemed to melt away, sliding onto the concrete floor and down one of the drains just as easy as running water.

"Because I wanted some time alone with you," Foster explained, "and I thought we could talk out here without as much pressure. Mom and Grandma will respect our privacy, most of the time, but they're too curious for that right now." Foster held Javi's hand and led him outside and around to the weaning pens where the younger cows learned to separate from their mothers. He leaned on the fencing, and a heifer walked over to him, huge eyes shining in the light from the barn.

"What's with this one?" The youngster stuck her head as close to Foster as she could.

"Her birth was hard and her mother rejected her, so I bottle-fed her. Now she's on grass and feed, but she thinks I'm her mother." Foster couldn't help petting her head. "She isn't the first one I've done that with, but I was feeling vulnerable, so I didn't separate as early as I should have. Now I think she'll be mine forever."

"Does she have a name?"

Foster blushed and hoped it was dark enough that Javi couldn't see. "Javita," he answered.

"You named a cow after me?" Javi said, and Foster couldn't tell if he was upset or not. Then he laughed. "So it's okay if I named one of the cockroaches that infested the place in Ohio after you?"

"I don't know about that." Now it was Foster's turn to laugh. "But she is cute and has great eyes like you." Foster was teasing, and thankfully Javi hugged him. "I came out here a lot while you were gone. It was quiet, and I listened to the cows as they ate and lowed. It was comforting and gave me time to think. But mostly what I did was miss you."

"There was a dairy herd in one of the fields next to where we were working, and every day I thought of you, wondering what you were doing at that moment. I kept seeing you in everything around me, and it hurt so badly." Javi kissed him gently at first. But when Foster parted his lips, heat built between them, and Foster slid his hands down Javi's back, pressing to his firm butt, bringing them as close as possible.

"Foster," his mother called from the back door. "Is everything all right?"

"Yes." *It would be a lot better if you'd leave me alone.*

She closed the door, and Foster chuckled, staying right where he was. It felt too good and right to stop. But they couldn't stay where they were forever. "Good night, Javita," Foster said to the cow and turned to Javi. "Let's go in." Together they walked hand in hand toward the house.

JAVI WAS still tired, so he went upstairs after saying good night and thanking Foster's mother for letting him stay. Once he was gone, she and Foster sat at the table for the conversation he was dreading.

"You want him to stay," she said, and Foster nodded. "I know he'll help out, and we could use it."

"Okay…," Foster said warily.

"And I know how you feel about him." Her speech was measured, fingers knitted together and hands resting on the table. "I'm not going to stand in your way. I want you to be happy." She reached out to touch his hand. "I also don't want you to get hurt, and I wonder what will happen if things between you don't work out."

"I know. Me too. But I have to see, and I can't do that if we send him on his way." Foster wanted Javi here with him more than he'd ever wanted or needed anything or anyone in his life.

"Then we'll see how things work out," she said, then paused. "I want you to understand that I'd have these same reservations if Javi were a girl. I don't want anyone to hurt my son."

Foster stood and walked around the table. "That's the nicest thing I think you could possibly have said, and it's all I'm asking for." He wrapped her in his arms from behind. "I love you, Mom."

"I love you too," she added cautiously and turned in her chair. "I expect…." The words trailed off, but her eyes said it all. Foster nodded and turned away. He knew that she was aware of what most likely was going to happen and was making it clear that she didn't want to hear or see… anything in the night.

Foster left his mother and went upstairs. He wondered if he should peer into Javi's room, but instead he went to his own, closed the door, and got undressed. He'd said that he'd wait for Javi, but now he wondered if he should go say good night and make sure Javi was okay.

Foster pulled on a pair of shorts, turned the knob, and opened the door to find Javi standing with his hand raised to knock.

"I wasn't sure…," Javi said and stepped inside.

"I didn't want to push you," Foster said as he closed the door. Javi stepped into his arms, and his doubts all slipped away. Foster tugged Javi's shirt over his head, stepping back to look at him. He was thinner but no less breathtaking. Foster slipped off his shorts and waited for Javi to do the same. Then he climbed in bed and held the covers open, waiting for Javi to decide what he wanted.

Javi didn't hesitate. He joined him in half a heartbeat, encircling Foster with his arms, holding him tightly as though he were something precious that had been lost and found again. He realized that was what he was to Javi and what he'd found. Javi had returned, and Foster intended to hold on as tightly as he could for as long as Javi would have him.

"I thought I'd never have this again," Foster whispered, holding Javi to him, sliding his hands over his smooth skin, avoiding his scars. "I want it all right now."

"I know. I can't believe I'm here at this moment with you. I keep thinking it's an illusion, and I'll blink and you'll be gone."

Foster rolled on top of Javi, chest to chest, hip to hip, their cocks nestled side by side, and stared down into Javi's eyes. "This is no illusion or dream. It's real and I want you forever." He closed the distance between their lips and started a night of passion that left them sore in all the right places, and hours later, just falling asleep, he held Javi to him and closed his eyes, looking forward to tomorrow.

Epilogue

Foster loved the spring. It was his favorite time of year. Everything from the pansies in the flowerbeds next to the back door, which his grandmother had already planted, to the livestock seemed to know that winter was over and that it was time for new life and new beginnings. It had also been his father's favorite time of year, and as Foster walked across the yard to the garden, he thought of his father and hoped he'd be proud of what he'd done and was doing.

"This thing is like riding a bull," Javi called from where he was tilling up new ground.

"Have you ever ridden a bull?" Foster shouted.

Javi stuck his tongue out before going back to his work. "I won't need to now."

"Yee-haw." Foster waved his hand over his head and watched as Javi laughed.

"You're supposed to be working, not joking around," his mother chastised with a slight smile.

"Yes, Mom," Foster deadpanned and pulled his drawing out of his pocket. "This is my plan for the garden. We're going to add eggplant, squash, small pumpkins for pie, and cabbage."

"What about tomatoes?"

"If you want a plant or two, go ahead, but we aren't going to sell them. I had thought about raspberries or blackberries, but they're too much trouble and too fragile to take efficiently to market. Do you agree?"

"Yes."

"Good. We'll plant in a few weeks, and when Javi is done over there, we'll spread fresh manure on the garden, till it in, and let the rain do its job. We should be able to plant seeds in a few weeks, with plants to follow." Foster looked up as his grandmother slowly made her way over using her cane. She'd fallen on ice during the winter and broken her left knee. They replaced it, and she was still strengthening it. Nothing stopped Grandma Katie, but she had slowed down some. "What do you think?"

"I think we're going to run out of land," she observed, and Foster smiled. "Not that it's a bad thing. You're putting it all to good use."

The engine on the tiller stopped and quiet surrounded them. "It's done," Javi said.

"Looks good," Grandma Katie said, giving Javi a thumbs-up. Javi and Foster's mother had had a slow start, but when his grandmother fell and broke her knee, she and Javi had been home alone, and he'd taken such good care of her that his mother had opened her heart to him. Foster had been thrilled—not at the broken-knee part, but that they had bonded. Javi already held his heart in so many ways.

Javi was covered in dirt and dust, but when he joined them, Foster kissed him right there. They were used to it by now. Others in town, well…. They'd had a few problems, but Foster figured it was time for them to put on their big-boy pants because he and Javi were here to stay.

When Foster released him, Javi moved to stand next to Grandma Katie. "Do you need to put your leg up?" Javi asked her.

Grandma Katie patted his hand. "I'm fine for now."

"Well, we're going to spread the manure, so you might want to go inside." The scent would be intense.

"Please, I've been around cow shit all my life. Besides, who's going to make sure you do it right?" She motioned them off, and Foster shook his head, handing his mother his plans. Then he and Javi went to get the wheelbarrows.

It took a good hour of hauling and spreading. Once that part was done, Foster had Javi start tilling it in while he continued hauling. Hard work was something he did all the time, but having Javi working with him made everything easier, even spreading manure.

By the time they were done and the manure was tilled in, Javi looked completely shaken up and ready to drop. "What's next?" he asked, as though he wasn't dog tired. That was one of the many things Foster had learned about Javi. He would work as long as there was work to do.

"Put the tiller back in the toolshed, and I'll take care of the rest of the equipment. Then we can get these boots and gloves off and wash up. I have a surprise for you." Foster grinned and hurried to put away the equipment. When he was done, Foster headed inside and went into the basement. He got a small cooler and went back upstairs. He washed up quickly and then filled the cooler with Cokes, because Javi loved them, and added ice from the freezer.

Javi met him out by the truck. Foster put the cooler inside, then they got in and pulled out of the drive.

"Where are we going?" Javi asked.

"You'll know in a few minutes." Foster made the turn and then started up the hill. They hadn't been up here since Javi returned. In the fall there was too much to do and then the snow had come, making climbing the hill impossible. But it was spring now, and he'd been aching to bring Javi here again.

They reached the top, and Foster parked. The wind was soft as it swirled around them, filled with warmth and promise. Foster grabbed the cooler and the blankets he'd stuffed behind the seat earlier in the day. He spread the blankets on the tailgate and motioned for Javi to hop up, putting the cooler behind them.

"Why here?" Javi asked, sitting next to Foster.

"This is a special spot, our spot. This is where I held you in my arms and you told me about yourself. Remember?" Javi nodded, and Foster slid back and then forward, sliding his legs around Javi, holding him. "Do you remember what you said then?"

"Not really," Javi answered.

"We stood like this with my arms around you, and I asked what your dreams were," Foster whispered.

Javi slid off the tailgate and turned, pushing Foster back as he kissed him. "I remember now." Javi tugged at Foster's shirt, undoing

168

the buttons and parting the fabric, stroking his chest while Foster groaned. He always loved being touched by Javi, who slid his hands down Foster's chest to his belly and kept going, opening his pants and pulling them down his legs.

"I wasn't expecting this…."

"I know. But if this spot is special, I want to make it extra special." Javi shucked his own clothes and pulled off Foster's shoes, then dropped his pants to the ground.

"Isn't it too cold?"

Javi climbed on top of him, and Foster wound his legs around Javi's waist. "You're always warm to me." Javi spit and wet himself before slowly sliding into Foster's body.

Foster groaned loud and long, making more noise than they dared at home.

"Scream for me. Let your shouts of love and ecstasy right out everywhere."

Foster didn't hold back, keening when Javi rubbed the spot inside, riding the waves of the heated stretch, enjoying the zing of pleasure and the warmth of Javi on top of him. Nothing ever compared to this—them together, alone, in a way only they were and ever would be.

The truck rocked with Javi's motions, and Foster groaned, wanting more, needing all Javi had to give him. "I feel you."

"Me too." Javi leaned forward and kissed the very center of Foster's chest. "I always feel you. When we're working I feel you, when we sleep, you're still there, and when we make love, I burn for you and only you." Foster was on the edge within seconds and climaxed right along with Javi seconds later with Javi in complete and wonderful control of his pleasure and body.

Neither of them moved until the haze of passion wore off and the lines on the truck bed dug into Foster's back. Javi backed away and stood, huffing heavily, watching him with half-lidded eyes.

"Wow," Foster murmured softly. "You were…."

"Too strong?" Javi asked.

"I was going to say amazing, memorable, awesome, and an animal, but those barely scratch the surface," Foster said with a satiated grin. The breeze picked up, and Foster shivered slightly. Javi picked up his clothes, and Foster placed them behind him, pulling one of the blankets up. Javi added his clothes to the pile in the truck and sat down. Foster spread a blanket over both of them, leaning in to kiss Javi, enjoying the quiet time with the man he loved more than anything.

"That day I brought you here, I asked you what your dreams were, remember?" Foster had never forgotten that day and Javi's answer. It was what he strove every day to change.

"I do." Javi leaned against him, finding Foster's hand under the blanket. "And I still don't have dreams. I allowed myself one, and it came true." Javi leaned close. "So I decided to take life as it comes and not press my luck."

"And what dream was that?" Foster asked, catching the hitch in his own voice.

"You."

Stay tuned for an excerpt from

The Lone Rancher

Dreamspun Desires

By Andrew Grey

He'll do anything to save the ranch, including baring it all.

Aubrey Klein is in real trouble—he needs some fast money to save the family ranch. His solution? A weekend job as a stripper at a club in Dallas. For two shows each Saturday, he is the star as The Lone Rancher.

It leads to at least one unexpected revelation: after a show, Garrett Lamston, an old friend from school, approaches the still-masked Aubrey to see about some extra fun… and Aubrey had no idea Garrett was gay. As the two men dodge their mothers' attempts to set them up with girls, their friendship deepens, and one thing leads to another.

Aubrey know his life stretching between the ranch and the club is a house of cards. He just hopes he can keep it standing long enough to save the ranch and launch the life—and the love—he really hopes he can have.

www.dreamspinnerpress.com

CHAPTER ONE

AUBREY KLEIN sat back in his chair with a groan. No matter how many ways he tried to add up these damned numbers, they just wouldn't come out right. The ranch was doing better, and he'd made a lot of progress in the last six months, but they were still hanging on by a lick and a prayer. The hole that had been dug in over years couldn't be filled in and wiped clean in a matter of months, he knew. The debt was going down, and if he had to, he could hold on for maybe another six months to a year, as long as he caught some sort of break with the weather. He closed the ledger with a thud and wished his daddy had converted the records to computer years ago. Of course, if he'd have done that, he might have done some of the other things necessary to keep the ranch from ending up on the brink of foreclosure.

"Son, are you done in there? I need your help in the yard."

"Sure, Dad, I'll be right there," Aubrey called. There was work to be done, and wishing the ranch books were in better shape wasn't going to make it happen. That was going to take hard work and sacrifice. Aubrey cringed as he thought about the sacrifices he'd already made. But if those sacrifices saved the ranch and helped his mom and dad get back on a level footing, it would be worth it.

He got up and left the office. For years this room had been his father's domain, but now it was his. Aubrey met his dad by the kitchen and followed him outside, where a load of hay for the horses was waiting to be unloaded. Aubrey groaned. "Where did this come from?" He clamped his eyes closed. They already had a barn full of hay.

"John Bridger had some extra, and we always need hay, so…."

"Dad." Aubrey stifled the urge to yell. It wouldn't do any good. Diabetes and its complications had slowly robbed his father of the ability to fully think things through, and he now tended to make emotional decisions as opposed to business or rational ones. "The barn's already full. There's enough hay to more than last us."

Dad walked to the barn and peered upward. Aubrey could see his father's shoulders slump slightly the moment he realized Aubrey was right, and just like that Aubrey wished he hadn't been. "Sorry, son, I thought…." His words trailed off in a cloud of defeat. "Nothing seems to turn out right for me anymore."

"Don't worry about it, Dad. I'll find a place for it. Just be sure to ask me before you buy things for the ranch. I have things under control, and we're going to be okay." Lord, he hoped to high heaven that he wasn't telling his dad a lie. Things were getting better, and he was close to having the money together to finally pay off the most vicious of the loans his father had taken out. Once that debt was gone, he hoped to be able to start paying down the others and free up some money for improvements. "Why don't you go on in and see what Mom has for lunch? I need to get this unloaded." Aubrey looked at his watch and realized he needed to get a move on, or he was going to be late.

"Everything okay?" Garrett Lamston asked as he came around the barn. He worked for Bridger and had obviously been the one to make the delivery. "You don't need this hay, do you?"

Aubrey waited until his dad was inside. "No. I have plenty right now. I know with the drought the past few months that there are plenty of folks who need it. But I—" The last thing he needed was another bill for something he didn't need.

"Don't you worry. John offered his extra to your dad because he wanted to make sure you had enough. We have a number of places that will take it." Garrett smiled, and Aubrey did his best not to let his heart do the little flips it always did when Garrett was nearby. Not that it mattered. He and Garrett were friends—or at least they'd known each other since they were kids. "It's not a problem."

"That's mighty good of you," Aubrey said with relief.

"I take it things are still tough for your dad." Garrett lifted his hat and wiped his forehead before dropping the old, once-white Stetson back down onto his head. He'd worn that same hat for years, and it looked as fine on him today as always.

"They aren't going to get better. All those years on insulin and not listening to the doctors have taken their toll. Momma does what she can, but he's a stubborn old coot and overdoes it all the time. Last week I found him passed out on the barn floor after he tried to clean stalls and overexerted himself." He'd had to use glucose injections to bring his father around. It hadn't been pretty, but he'd done what he had to.

Garrett nodded slowly in that way he had. "Wish there was something I could do to help."

Aubrey patted the trailer. "You already have."

Garrett smiled and turned to go. Aubrey watched him as he went, glad he was alone, because anyone watching him stare at that high, pert cowboy ass in those tight Wranglers would know exactly what kind of thoughts and images were running around in his head. He blinked to clear his lascivious thoughts and school his expression as Garrett climbed in the truck. While things were changing—maybe slowly in this part of Texas—he wasn't about to tempt fate and let everyone know which way he swung. With the ranch just hanging on, the last thing he needed was rumors and folks deciding they didn't need to be doing business with him. That could be the end of everything he'd been working so hard to preserve.

Aubrey raised his hand in a combination farewell and thank-you. Garrett opened the window, leaning out so Aubrey got a look at just his head and broad shoulders. "We should go for a beer sometime. Give me a call the next time you're going to town, and I'll meet you."

"I'll buy the first round," Aubrey called and swallowed hard as Garrett stared back at him for a second longer than necessary. Heat rose in Aubrey's stomach as that itchy feeling filled his belly and the tingle of potential possibilities buzzed in his head. He blinked and was about to turn away when Garrett pulled his head back into the truck and thunked the door closed. A hand jutted out the window, and the truck and trailer started pulling down the drive. Aubrey inhaled deeply, wondering if he'd really seen what he thought. It had to be his imagination. He'd known Garrett for years, and there had never been any indication in all that time that Garrett was interested in bulls rather than heifers.

With one small crisis averted, Aubrey pulled his attention away from the possible contents of Garrett's jeans and turned toward the house.

"Did you get the hay unloaded already?" his dad asked from his favorite recliner in the living room when Aubrey got out of the oppressive heat and into the air-conditioned comfort of the house.

"Bridger offered it to us because he wanted to make sure we were doing okay. There are other folks who need it a lot worse, so they're going to sell it to them." He patted his dad's shoulder lightly. "We're going to be okay, and it's all good."

"Okay, then…." His dad put his feet up, and Aubrey figured he'd probably be asleep in five minutes or less.

"You ready to eat?" his mom asked as she came in from the kitchen. She'd aged a lot over the past few years, just like his dad. Her hair was mostly gray now instead of the raven black he remembered from when he was younger. Unlike his father, she was in good health, but taking care of Dad had taken its toll on her.

"That'd be great. I need to leave in an hour or so." He checked his watch.

"Going to Dallas again to see your friends?" she asked without judgment or reproach.

"Yeah." He sat at the table and hung his hat on the back of the chair next to him.

"You need to get away every now and then. Everything here will be fine while you're gone." She got plates and dished up some of her special macaroni salad and added a huge, thick sandwich on homemade bread. None of that store-bought "sawdust bread," as she called it. Mom did things the old-fashioned way whenever she could, but it was getting harder and harder on her. All Aubrey wanted to do was make his mom and dad's lives easier, and he'd do whatever he had to in order to make that happen.

"This is really good," he told her, not really wanting to talk too much about his weekly trips into Dallas to see his "friends." The less he said, the fewer lies he told, and when it came to his momma, that was always a good thing. "You always take good care of us." He took another bite of the roast beef sandwich and sighed to himself.

"You're the one taking care of us now," she said. She looked into the other room.

"Did he eat?"

"Yeah. He was hungry, so I fed him as soon as he came in," she whispered. "He ate, then went to sit in his chair and fell asleep." She turned away and sat down with her own plate. His mom had always been the last one to eat. "I heard from Carolann this morning. She said she's been real busy in San Francisco with her work and all."

Aubrey nodded and tried not to let jealousy and bitterness well up. His sister always had excuses not to come home and help out. Aubrey took another bite of his sandwich to stifle a growl. Part of the reason they were all in this mess was because his dad had taken out a loan against the ranch to help pay for her Stanford education.

"She said she sent out a check to start paying us back."

Aubrey lowered his head and tried not to humph. Somehow the postal service always seemed to lose Carolann's checks. "That's good." There was no use arguing. Mom wouldn't hear it. Carolann was her only daughter, just like he was her only son, and Momma wasn't going to hear bad things said about either of her children. Besides, Aubrey knew the loan had been their decision, and what was done was done. "When I get back, I'm going to put in that new electric line out to the barn. That way I can bury the cable and get rid of that old overhead line."

"You need me to do anything for you while you're gone?"

"Just make sure Dad feeds and waters the horses. I got everything set out in the barn, so it'll be easy on him. He needs to do it tonight and tomorrow morning. I'll be back in the afternoon and can take over from there."

She flashed him a disgusted look. "We've been doing this work for—"

Aubrey put up his hand to keep her from getting up a head of steam. "I was only trying to help." Aubrey looked to the living room. "He bought a trailer load of hay we didn't need," he added in a whisper. "I took care of it, but I'm worried."

The fire in her eyes died. "I am too." Her voice was little more than a whisper and filled with pain and worry. He hated the strain all this was taking on her. "We'll take care of things here." She took his plate when he was done. "Go on and have some fun. You work hard, so you deserve it. Give yourself a chance to let off some steam with your friends, and I'll see you tomorrow."

Aubrey stood and kissed his mom on the cheek. Then he strode down to his room and grabbed the small bag he had packed and ready. He carried it out to his truck and then did one last check that everything was all set before he got in the truck and pulled down the drive for the ride from Greenville to Dallas.

ANDREW GREY grew up in western Michigan with a father who loved to tell stories and a mother who loved to read them. Since then he has lived all over the country and traveled throughout the world. He has a master's degree from the University of Wisconsin-Milwaukee and now works full-time on his writing. Andrew's hobbies include collecting antiques, gardening, and leaving his dirty dishes anywhere but in the sink (particularly when writing). He considers himself blessed with an accepting family, fantastic friends, and the world's most supportive and loving husband. Andrew currently lives in beautiful historic Carlisle, Pennsylvania.

E-mail: andrewgrey@comcast.net
Website: www.andrewgreybooks.com

BETWEEN LOATHING AND LOVE

ANDREW GREY

Theatrical agent Payton Gowan meets with former classmate—and prospective client—Beckett Huntington with every intention of brushing him off. Beckett not only made high school a living hell for Payton, but he was also responsible for dashing Payton's dreams of becoming a Broadway star.

Aspiring actor Beckett Huntington arrives in New York City on a wing and a prayer, struggling to land his first gig. He knows scoring Payton Gowan as an agent would be a great way to get his foot in the door, but with their history, getting the chance is going to be a tough sell.

Against Payton's better judgment, he agrees to give Beckett a chance, only to discover—to his amazement—that Beckett actually does have talent.

Payton signs Beckett but can't trust him—until Payton's best friend, Val, is attacked. When Beckett is there for him, Payton begins to see another side to his former bully. Amidst attempts by a jealous agent to sabotage Beckett's career and tear apart their blossoming love, Payton and Beckett must learn to let go of the past if they have any chance at playing out a future together.

www.dreamspinnerpress.com

EYES
ONLY ME
FOR

ANDREW GREY

For years, Clayton Potter's been friends and workout partners with Ronnie. Though Clay is attracted, he's never come on to Ronnie because, let's face it, Ronnie only dates women.

When Clay's father suffers a heart attack, Ronnie, having recently lost his dad, springs into action, driving Clay to the hospital over a hundred miles away. To stay close to Clay's father, the men share a hotel room near the hospital, but after an emotional day, one thing leads to another, and straight-as-an-arrow Ronnie make a proposal that knocks Clay's socks off! Just a little something to take the edge off.

Clay responds in a way he's never considered. After an amazing night together, Clay expects Ronnie to ignore what happened between them and go back to his old life. Ronnie surprises him and seems interested in additional exploration. Though they're friends, Clay suddenly finds it hard to accept the new Ronnie and suspects that Ronnie will return to his old ways. Maybe they both have a thing or two to learn.

www.dreamspinnerpress.com

FIRE AND Rain

ANDREW GREY

Carlisle Cops: Book Three

Since the death of their mother, Josten Applewhite has done what he's had to do to take care of his little brother and keep their small family together. But in an instant, a stroke of bad luck tears down what little home he's managed to build, and Jos and Isaac end up on the streets.

That's where Officer Kip Rogers finds them, and even though he knows he should let the proper authorities handle things, he cannot find it in his heart to turn them away, going so far as to invite them to stay in his home until they get back on their feet. With the help of Kip and his friends, Jos starts to rebuild his life. But experience has taught him nothing comes for free, and the generosity seems too good to be true—just like everything about Kip.

Kip's falling hard for Jos, and he likes the way Jos and Isaac make his big house feel like a home. But their arrangement can't be permanent, not with Jos set on making his own way. Then a distant relative emerges, determined to destroy Jos's family, and Kip knows Jos needs him—even if he's not ready to admit it.

www.dreamspinnerpress.com

ANDREW GREY

LOVE COMES
TO *Light*

A Senses Series Story

Artist Arik Bosler is terrified he might have lost his creative gift in the accident that left his hand badly burned. When he's offered the chance to work with renowned artist Ken Brighton, Arik fears his injury will be too much to overcome.

He travels to Pleasanton to meet Ken, where he runs into the intimidating Reg Thompson. Reg, a biker who customizes motorcycles, is a big man with a heart of gold who was rejected by most of his family. Arik is initially afraid of Reg because of his size. However it's Reg's heart that warms Arik's interest and gets him to look past the exterior to let down his guard.

But Arik soon realizes that certain members of Reg's motorcycle club are into things he can't have any part of. Reg can't understand why Arik disappears until he learns Arik's injury was the result of his father's drug activity. Though neither Reg nor Arik wants anything to do with drugs, the new leadership of Reg's club might have other ideas.

www.dreamspnnerpress.com

ROUND
AND
ROUND

ANDREW GREY

Sequel to *Backward*
Bronco's Boys: Book Four

When it comes to love, Kevin Foster can't seem to win. Some consider him a hero, but dousing an arsonist's attempt to burn Bronco's to the ground puts Kevin on the vengeful criminal's radar. Afterward, the arsonist fixates on Kevin, determined to burn away every part of Kevin's life.

Coming to Kevin's rescue more than once, and in more ways than one, is "MacDreamy Hotness"—firefighter Angus MacTavish. Not only is Angus smitten at first sight, he learns Kevin's nickname for him, intriguing him further.

When Angus discovers Kevin is the arsonist's target, he takes it upon himself to protect him at any cost. Soon Kevin works his way into a heart Angus thought he'd closed off for good. Things heat up between them, but the arsonist has no intention of letting Kevin finally find happiness. Hopefully Angus and Kevin can stop him before he reduces everything Kevin values to ash—including the love igniting between him and Angus.

www.dreamspinnerpress.com

CPSIA information can be obtained
at www.ICGtesting.com
Printed in the USA
LVHW040111280323
742794LV00014B/950